Heart of the Hunted

Georgina Stancer

Editing by Stacey Jaine McIntosh

Cover design by EmCat & Butterfly Designs

For Joe.
You will forever live on in the hearts and minds of the
people who had the pleasure of knowing you.
We miss you always.

Prologue
Natalia

"What are you doing here?" Natalia jumped at the sound of her mother's voice coming from behind her.

"I... I wanted to...to..." she stuttered.

"You shouldn't be here," her mother said sternly.

"I'm sorry, I just wanted... I was worried..."

Pulling Natalia in for a tight hug, her mother stroked her hair and said "I'm okay, Natalia, but it's not safe for you out here."

"I know. I'm sorry, Mummy ."

"It's okay this time, but don't do it again, okay?"

"Okay, I promise."

"Good girl," she said smiling down at her. "Now, stay close to me, okay?"

"Okay."

Natalia followed closely behind her mother as they quietly made their way around the abandoned building, looking for her mother's friend.

"Don't make a sound," her mother whispered.

Nodding, Natalia held her breath, thinking it would help her hear better. It didn't. It just made her heart beat even louder in her ears.

Without warning her mother grabbed hold of her hand and started running. Natalia tried her hardest to keep up with her, but her little legs just couldn't go as fast as her mother's longer legs.

All but dragging her out of the building, they headed straight for the woodlands surrounding the building. Natalia tripped on the uneven ground several times, and she would have fallen on her face if her mother hadn't been holding her hand.

Natalia knew she was slowing her mother down, but instead of complaining or leaving her behind, her mother stopped just long enough to pick her up so she could carry her.

"Don't look back," her mother said as she started running again.

Natalia held on tightly as her mother ran as fast as she could, tucking her head into her mother's neck so she couldn't see behind them.

It didn't take long for her mother to start slowing. Natalia was a big girl now, she was nearly seven years old, so she knew it was her fault her mother couldn't keep up the pace.

Panting heavily, her mother stopped and lowered Natalia to the ground.

"Stay here, Natalia," she told her, pushing her into a hollowed-out tree. "And don't move until I come back for you."

"But Mummy..."

"No buts, Natalia. Stay here and stay silent."

"Okay," Natalia whispered.

Without another word, her mother ran off, leaving her all alone in the middle of the woods. Natalia knew why her mother did it, but that didn't help the fear from gnawing at her stomach. Fear for herself, but mostly for her mother. She knew her mother was leading the monsters away from her.

She knew it was her fault they had been spotted, even without her mother saying so. If she hadn't followed her mother out of the bunker, then the monsters wouldn't have seen them.

Natalia knew she shouldn't leave the bunker, she knew it was too dangerous outside, but she wanted to be useful... she wanted to make sure her mother was safe.

Natalia thought it was safer for her outside than her mother. The monsters didn't kill children, only the adults of her kind... Human kind... but never children. No, they had a far worse fate for children. Which was why Natalia's mother was desperately trying to lead them away.

Natalia hunkered down in her hiding spot, determined not to give herself away. Listening intently, all she could hear was the sound of leaves rustling in the wind and the beating of her heart in her ears.

She didn't know how long she had to wait for her mother to return, but she hoped it wasn't too much longer. It was getting darker and colder as time passed.

Yawning, Natalia curled up into a ball at the base of the tree, trying to warm herself as the temperature dropped and night fell with still no sign of her mother returning for her.

Natalia waited hours, but she couldn't keep her eyes open any longer. Sending up a silent prayer that her mother would return for her soon, Natalia closed her eyes and fell asleep, cold and alone.

CHAPTER ONE

Taredd

"What's on your mind?" Dain asked.

"Just thinking about the Humans," Taredd told him.

Two hundred years had passed since the Humans eyes were opened to the world around them, and to the creatures hiding in plain sight. When the war broke out between the supernatural races, it was the best thing that could have ever happen to this magical place.

New life sprung forth as the buildings Humans built crumbled to the ground. Mother Nature was slowly taking back her home once more. Well, except for some of the small towns and villages the supernatural races have commandeered for themselves, those were thriving.

Taredd had no sympathy for the Humans, they didn't deserve to call this place home, not when they were slowly killing it. He remembered all too well the destruction they left in their wake when they were left to rule this land, so he was glad they were nearly extinct.

Vile, despicable creatures the lot of them. Which

was why after the war ended, he eagerly hunted down the last remaining Humans, killing the adults and capturing the children to sell on to slavers.

The Humans thought they could hide away from the world when the war broke out. They thought if they hid then they could escape the punishment they deserved. Little did they know, it didn't matter how well they hid themselves, they were going to be caught.

Once, there were billions of them. Now, Taredd guessed there were fewer than a hundred left. He planned on making sure that none survived.

"Why the fuck would you want to think about them? Just enjoy your night off for once. They will still be there for you to hunt tomorrow," Dain said.

"Hopefully not for too much longer," Taredd told him.

"I'll drink to that," Arun said as he raised his glass.

Dain and Arun had been by his side since long before the war started. They had each other's backs no matter the situation. It was always them against the world, and yet, they were the most unlikely of allies.

A Demon, a Shapeshifter, and a Fae. It sounds more like the beginning of a really bad joke, but they were closer than brothers. Nothing could tear them apart, not even others of their own kind.

When the war broke out and their own kinds wanted them to fight against each other, they stuck together, refusing to fight any species except for the Humans. After all, it was the Humans that needed terminating, not any of the other races.

Now the three of them worked together, using their individual skills to hunt down and kill any remaining Human adults and rounding up the children.

"So why think about them now?" Dain asked. "After the week we've had, we deserve the night off."

It had been a productive week. Between the three of them they had managed to track down and capture sixteen Humans. Six of which were just children, one of them being a baby. Because none of them could bring themselves to kill a child, even a Human one, they collected them up and sold them to slavers.

Some of the children managed to stay hidden from them. Taredd wasn't concerned for those ones because most didn't survive on their own. The lucky few that did make it to adulthood, were then hunted down just like the rest. Either way, it was one less Human to worry about.

"Yeah, that's true," Taredd agreed.

"I think we deserve longer than a night off," Arun said.

"A week sounds good," Dain said. "Since we're our own boss, why don't we take a week off?"

"You two can if you want to, but I would rather have the time off when we're done," Taredd told them.

"It's been years since we had more than a night off, don't you think it's about time we did?" Arun asked.

"As I said, you two can if you want, but I'm going to carry on for a bit longer. I don't think there's many of them left."

"All the more reason to have a break," Dain said.

"All the more reason to carry on," he countered.

"You know how fast they reproduce."

"Yeah, I do, and it's not that bloody fast. It's not as if they breed like rodents," Dain said.

"Thankfully," Taredd added.

"If that was the case, then we would be fighting a losing battle," Arun said. "But we're not. They are nearly all gone as you well know. So, I'm with Dain, we need a break. Even if it's just for a couple of days."

They were right and Taredd knew it. They had worked tirelessly since the end of the war, so they did deserve to have some time off, but Taredd could see the light at the end of the tunnel. It wouldn't be long until the Humans were completely wiped from the face of the planet. Well, except for the children.

The children were a different matter entirely. Depending on who they were sold to, depended on their fate. Most were slaves, sold to serve their master. Some were used as food, either for their blood or to eat their meat.

Taredd didn't see the appeal in either. He wasn't one for keeping slaves anyway, he would rather have employees than slaves because they were loyal if they were treated well, and the thought of eating a child turned his stomach.

"Fine. A couple of days, but that's it," he gave in.

"That's all we're asking for," Arun said.

"You, maybe. I was after longer," Dain sulked.

"Think yourself lucky you're having that much time," Taredd told him.

"Think yourself lucky I'm still helping after all these years," Dain countered.

"You bitch and moan, but you wouldn't be anywhere else," Arun said.

"Yeah, true. Only because I'd be bored. You guys are so fucking entertaining when you're hunting." Dain laughed. "It's like watching young Shapeshifters hunt in animal form for the first time."

"You must be talking about yourself, as usual," Arun told him. "I am by far the more superior hunter out of the three of us."

This time Taredd laughed as well. Out of the three of them, Arun was the least equipped for hunting... anything. Yes, being Fae meant he had magic, but that didn't necessarily mean he was better at hunting.

Taredd hated to admit it, but out of the three of them, Dain was the better hunter. It helped that he could call upon the enhanced senses of the animals he turned into. If it wasn't for that ability, then Taredd would be the best.

After all, Demons were capable of many things, and.... not boasting or anything... he was far superior than most of his own kind as well.

"You seriously think you're better?" Arun asked him.

"Then you? Hell, yes," Taredd said bluntly.

"How much do you want to bet?"

"Oooh, interesting," Dain said, rubbing his hands together. "Can I get in on the action?"

"Why not," Arun said. "So, what's it going to be?"

"How about, the first to capture a Human...." he trailed off, making it appear he was thinking hard about what to bet.

"What?" Dain asked impatiently.

"The first to capture a Human gets fifty gold pieces," Taredd said.

"I don't know about that," Arun said.

"That's because you know I'm the better hunter."

"Either that, or he's a chicken," Dain said.

"I am not poultry," Arun said indignantly.

"So, I'm the better hunter then?" Taredd asked.

"Fine," Arun gave in. "Fifty gold pieces it is then."

"Exciting. I can't wait to see who wins. Now, the question is, which one of you do I bet on?" Dain asked, tapping his finger against his chin.

"That would be me," Arun told him.

"Only if you want to lose your money as well," Taredd said confidently.

"I think I'll go with... urm..."

"Seriously?" Arun said. "Just fucking pick one of us!"

"No need to be so testy," Dain said. "I'll go with Taredd to win."

"Oh, I see how it is," Arun told them. "You'll both be out of pocket when I win."

"That's if you win," Dain said.

"Oh, I will, and it will be more money for me when I do," he said smugly.

"Anyway, when do you want to start the bet?" Taredd asked, knowing what the answer would be before Arun even opened his mouth.

"There's no time like the present, don't you think," Arun said, confirming Taredd's suspicion.

"You want to start it now?" When Arun nodded,

Taredd added. "I thought you wanted a couple of days off?"

"I'll have a better time off when I've got one hundred gold pieces burning a hole in my pocket."

"Fine. It begins now, then." Taredd agreed.

At the end of the day he wasn't going to complain, they were still going to be hunting. He would rather they worked as a group, but anything was better than nothing.

"Right, I'll see you both later. I've got a Human to hunt and a bet to win," Arun said before downing the last of his drink. Placing his empty glass on the counter, he stood and said, "See you two later." Then walked off.

"Do you think he's going to win?" Dain asked.

"No chance," Taredd said, shaking his head. "You've seen him hunting, do you really think he stands a chance against me?"

"Yeah, true. It's just, he seems more confident than I thought he would be."

Taredd knew exactly what Dain meant. If Taredd didn't know better, he would have thought Arun already knew where a Human was hiding. It was the only thing he could think off that would make Arun seem so confident. But no, it wasn't like Arun to cheat, and it would be cheating if he already knew where to find one.

"Nah, I think it's all an act. Arun knows I'm the better hunter, whether he wants to admit it or not."

"It's a good job he's not betting against me. At least with you he might stand a very slim chance of winning." Dain said, laughing.

Taredd didn't bother replying to that. Instead, he downed the last of his drink and stood to leave as well.

"I'm off to bed," Taredd told him. "I want to get an early start in the morning."

"I can't believe you're cutting out early as well," Dain sulked.

"Would you rather I let Arun win?" Taredd asked with one brow raised.

"Oh, hell no. I would rather stick red hot pokers in my eyes than let him win," Dain said. "Can you imagine how annoying he would be if he did?"

"Exactly. So, it's best if I get an early-ish... night."

"Yeah, point made. Go to bed because I really don't want to give my gold to Arun."

Shaking his head, Taredd walked away. He wouldn't be surprised if Dain spent the rest of the night in the tavern. Even if Taredd didn't have the bet going with Arun, he didn't want to spend the rest of the night here. If anything, the bet gave him a good excuse to leave early.

He didn't have to go far to reach the motel where he was staying the night. It was a rundown place, but it had a bed and a place for him to wash, so it would do for the time being.

Climbing the stairs in the ratty old building, Taredd debated on whether to start the hunt tonight or wait until the morning. Stopping briefly outside Arun's room, he waited to see if he was still here. Taredd didn't hear anything, but that didn't mean Arun had already left. He could just be sleeping.

Deciding to stay the night and start fresh in the morning, Taredd carried on to his room further along the corridor. Even if Arun had begun hunting tonight, Taredd was happy to let him have a head start. After all, he was going to need all the advantage he could get if he was going to beat Taredd.

Closing the door behind him, Taredd made a beeline for the bed... or what passed for a bed around here. It wasn't the cleanest place in the world, far from it. Taredd could imagine it was probably a nice place to stay at one point, but that was many years ago.

Kicking his boots off, he sat on the end of the bed and looked around the room. Shitty as it was, it would do for the night. Tomorrow would be here soon enough and it was looking like it was going to be a long assed day, so tonight he was going to get as much rest as he could.

CHAPTER TWO

Natalia

"We can stay one more night, but that's it," Amberly said.

"Yeah, I know," Natalia told her.

Amberly had been Natalia's best friend since they were young children. Natalia couldn't remember which one of them joined their group first, but she was glad they met. Being the same age, they'd grown up more like sisters.

As much fun as it was to spend all day every day with your best friend, being on the run constantly was no way to live life. Moving from one shitty bunker to the next. Natalia was fed up of never being able to stay in one place longer than a few nights, but that had been every Humans way of life since before she was born, ever since the Great War.

Unless she was able to build a time machine, like the ones she had read about in some of the books she found occasionally when she was out scavenging for supplies, it was likely to be that way for the rest of her life.

When Natalia was younger, she used to dream she

was one of the characters she'd read about. The dreams never lasted long though. Real life would always come crashing down on her before too long.

If only she had been born before the Great War, when life was simple and easy. Back then, nobody knew that the monsters they read about in books were actually real. They soon found out differently when the Great War started.

Everything from Demons to Shapeshifters and Vampires to Fae, it was all real. What was worse, they were all out for blood…Human blood.

From what Natalia had been told about the time of the Great War, more than half of the Human population were killed in less than a week. The rest of Humanity scattered, trying to stay out of the way of a war that had nothing to do with them. Some succeeded, otherwise she wouldn't be here today, but most weren't so lucky.

Within a year, the majority of Humanity had been wiped from the face of the planet. It wasn't any better once the war was over either, as those that survived were then hunted down and killed mercilessly.

Nowadays, the last few remaining Humans alive travelled in small groups. Not only was it safer to travel with others, but the groups were kept small so they weren't as easily seen. The smaller the group the better, but it needed to be more than four to be on the safe side.

Natalia remembered a time when there was over thirty people in their group, now there was less than half left. Over the years the numbers had dwindled drastically in their group. So much so that if their luck didn't change soon, then there would be none of them left.

"Donovan's cooking dinner tonight," Amberly told her.

"It should be edible then," Natalia said.

Not everyone they travelled with could cook. Many a times Natalia and Amberly had come down with food poisoning. It was that bad at one point, Natalia had refused to eat anything that was cooked by anyone other than herself, Amberly, or Donovan. At least they knew how to cook properly, unlike nearly everyone else.

Not long after the last bout of food poisoning... which lasted nearly a week... Amberly took it upon herself to teach everyone who couldn't cook how to. Now most of them could cook at least simple meals, with the exception of Rafe. It didn't matter how much time Amberly spent teaching him, he didn't seem to get it. So, whenever it was his turn, Natalia went without.

"Has everyone returned?" Natalia asked.

"All but two," Amberly said.

"Shit! It's nearly dark," Natalia said worriedly. "They should have been back by now."

"Rafe wants to go looking for them," Amberly said.

Natalia's head snapped up at the news. "I hope someone stopped him? It's not safe at night."

"You don't need to tell me," Amberly said, raising her eyebrows. "I know just how dangerous it is."

"Did the others at least come back with anything?"

she asked.

The whole point in them going out in the first place was to scavenge whatever they could, whether it was for food, clothing, weapons, or whatever else they needed to survive. If they came back empty handed, then they would have lost another two people for nothing. Not that they should be losing people full stop, but there was nothing she could do to change that, and at the end of the day they needed the supplies. So they had no choice but to risk lives.

"Yeah, they managed to pick up a few bits. Not nearly enough though," Amberly said.

The problem was, they had to venture close to the creatures that were trying to kill them in order to stock up on supplies. There was nothing else left from their own kind, it had all been looted long before she was born.

"Fingers crossed the others will be back soon," Natalia said.

"If they don't, we're going to be down another two people," Amberly sighed.

Grimacing, Natalia said "I know, it's not great, but we'll manage... somehow."

"What we need to do, is find more people," Amberly said.

It was easier said than done nowadays. The Human race was rapidly dwindling, and there was nothing anyone could do about it. Well, it would help if they weren't being hunted down and killed, but she didn't think the monsters...as she liked to call them...were going to stop until there wasn't any of them left.

"I don't think that's going to happen any time soon. How long has it been since we last came across anyone?" Natalia asked.

"At least three years," Amberly told her.

Natalia hadn't thought it had been that long, but thinking about it, it must have been.

"Maybe we need to move further away. Didn't the last group say they were heading up north?" Amberly asked.

"Something like that. We need a plan though," Natalia said. "I don't think just heading north is a good idea. I don't think anyone here has been up there before."

"I think you're right," Amberly agreed. "I haven't heard any of the others talking about it."

Natalia, Amberly, and Donovan were the only ones left from their original group. Everyone else had joined up with them later on along the way. Most of them came from the same group, which was why so many of them couldn't cook when they first joined.

It made Natalia wonder about the other group. How any of them survived this far without knowing basic survival skills such as cooking was beyond her. Did any of their previous group know how to cook? If so, why didn't they teach everyone else?

It was one of the first things they were taught growing up... that and how to stay hidden. There was no point learning how to fight when the creatures you were up against had magic, razor sharp claws and teeth, or the ability to transform into anything they could imagine. Not to mention they were all incredibly stronger than Humans, no matter what race they were.

It would be like an ant fighting against a Human. Hands down, the Human would win every time, which was exactly the same as fighting against the creatures. Even the seemingly weak among them could easily over power a Human without much effort.

"We'll talk about what to do next over dinner. Let the others know that it's time to move on tomorrow," Natalia said.

"I've done it already," Amberly said. "They're waiting to hear what the plan is."

"Dinner's in five minutes," Donovan said, sticking his head around the corner.

"Great, we'll be there in a minute," Amberly told him.

Donovan nodded before leaving as quickly as he entered.

"Well, they won't have to wait long," Natalia pointed out.

"I must admit, I'll be glad to finally be out of this bunker," Amberly said after a moment.

"You could have gone with the others today," Natalia told her.

"I know," she said. "But it's not the same with them."

"I know what you mean," Natalia agreed.

Natalia and Amberly worked well together. They could easily read each other's body language and hand gestures, which was essential when on a supply run. You couldn't always count on being able to communicate verbally. So, working with people who couldn't read you and you couldn't read them was not the best of ideas.

It was also an extremely bad idea to go it alone. You needed someone to watch your back and vice-versa.

"Are you feeling better at least?" Amberly asked.

"Yeah, my head's finally stopped pounding," Natalia said, relieved it had gone. "That remedy we found the other week worked wonders."

"That's good. Make sure to write it down in the book," Amberly said.

"I will do."

Their book was currently just a few folded pieces of paper slid between the pages of a medicine book they found. The medicine book was from before the great war. Most of it they didn't understand, but it gave them the idea to start their own book. So now they were on the lookout for an empty book to fill themselves.

It wasn't something they shared with the rest of the group though. Donovan knew about it, but he was the only person other than Natalia and Amberly.

"Anyway, let's go and eat before Donovan shouts at us for letting it go cold," Amberly said.

"You go ahead," Natalia told her. "I'll be through in a minute."

"Okay, see you in there," she said on her way out.

Once Natalia was alone again, she opened her satchel and pulled out the book in question. She wanted to write it down before she forgot. They were fast running out of space on the paper, it wouldn't be long before they needed a new one.

The problem with that, was it's not something they

came across often. All three of them looked for a book to use whenever they were scavenging, but so far nothing. They couldn't ask the others to keep an eye out for one without telling them why, which none of them were prepared to do.

It wasn't that they didn't trust the others, they wouldn't be traveling with them if it was a matter of trust. You couldn't survive this life if you didn't have any trust in the people you were with. It wasn't even that they wanted to keep the remedies to themselves, either. They were more than happy to share the information, they just didn't want the others touching their book.

None of them wanted to lose it or for it to get ruined in any way, but the more people who had access to it, the more likely something like that was going to happen. Not only that, but the three of them started it together long before they met up with the others in the group, and they wanted to keep it between just the three of them.

A pencil was their only means to write. It wasn't the most reliable way, since it often faded from overuse and disappeared completely when the paper was wet, but it was all they had. Natalia knew people used to use things called pens, but none of the ones they found had worked.

Natalia copied word for word onto the paper, before returning it to the book. Natalia put it all back in her satchel when she was finished. Leaving the satchel on the pile of blankets she was using as a bed, Natalia stood and stretched before joining the others for dinner.

"What took you so long?" Donovan asked as she sat down. "Your dinner is nearly cold."

"Sorry, I was just packing up ready for tomorrow," she lied. Later she'll tell him what she was doing, but for now, that was all she was going to say.

"Amberly said we're moving on tomorrow," Rafe said.

"What if the others aren't back by then?" Bella asked.

"Then we'll leave them," Natalia told her.

"Why can't we wait? Or better yet, go looking for them?" Bella asked.

"You know why. If we wait, we stand more chance of being caught, and you know we don't go looking for missing people. If we did and they've been caught, then we would likely be caught as well. It's this way so the majority of the group stays safe," Natalia reminded her, "Which is why whenever we go out, we go in pairs and not as a whole group. It's bad enough moving between camps when we're all together."

"Yeah, I know. It just doesn't seem right to leave without them," Bella said.

"I know. I wish there was more we could do, but there isn't," Natalia said, shaking her head. "So, we have to go on without them."

"So, where are we going next?" Rafe asked.

"Amberly mentioned heading north. We don't know what's up there, but after thinking about it, I agree with her," Natalia said. When they all moaned, she added, "Does anyone have a better idea? If so, I'd like to hear it."

When nobody piped up with a better idea, Natalia said: "That's settled then. We'll leave at first light, so get plenty of rest after dinner, if you can."

Natalia hoped she was making the right decision in heading north, but only time would tell. For now, she was going to try to follow her own advice, and get plenty of rest. Tomorrow was going to be a long day.

CHAPTER THREE

Taredd

Taredd wasn't surprised to find that Arun had left early the next morning. For someone who wanted time off, he was awfully eager to get going with the hunt. Taredd wondered if there was more to it than Arun just wanting to win a bet, but he wasn't about to pry into Arun's private life. Arun was welcome to his secrets. He knew if he ever needed them, Taredd and Dain would be there, no matter what.

Dain was more than likely still fast asleep at this hour. He probably only turned in an hour or so ago, so it'll be closer to lunch time before he finally crawled out of his pit. Either way, it didn't matter to Taredd. Neither he nor Arun would accept any help from the Shapeshifter. After all, that would be cheating.

Taredd packed up his few belongings, then headed out. The sooner he found a Human, the sooner the bet would be over with and they could all get back to work. Yes, technically he was still working, but they were much more efficient when they were all on the same team, working together rather than against each other.

Stepping outside, Taredd took a deep breath of the fresh morning air. This was the best time of day to start a hunt. Humans seemed to think they had nothing to worry about in the day, especially first thing in the morning. They thought it was more dangerous at night, so they let their guard down in the day. Which was a huge mistake on their part. In fact, it was more dangerous during the day. Taredd wasn't about to enlighten them to the fact though, because it made his job a hell of a lot easier.

Without a destination in mind, Taredd decided to head north. He didn't know why he picked that direction, as it wasn't very popular with the Humans because of the colder climates. Only a few had been caught up there over the last ten or so years. But for some reason, Taredd had a feeling it was the right place to begin his search.

The cold weather didn't bother him. Like many of the other species, he could regulate his body temperature using magic. The Shapeshifters were the only kind unable to do that, but then they could transform into an animal that could withstand the cold so they didn't need the ability.

The weather wasn't all that great where he was at the moment either. It was prone to rain an awful lot, and the wind could pick up without a moment's notice. But a couple of miles up the road, it was even worse. At this time of the year it snowed regularly.

The mountains didn't help either. More often than not they were covered with snow, just like they were today. From where Taredd had been staying, to travel north meant he would have to pass through the mountains first.

This is where it would be handy to transform into another creature, but unfortunately his kind couldn't transform into anything else like some of the other species could. If he had possessed that ability, he would have turned into a bird and covered the distance in a third of the time. But since he couldn't, he was stuck with walking on two legs. At least he was faster on his feet than Arun.

Taredd wondered how Arun was getting on with his search. Which direction had he taken? Knowing Arun, he was more than likely heading back down south. Even though he could regulate his temperature the same as Taredd, he still preferred the warmer climates. So Taredd wouldn't put it passed him to head in that direction. Whether or not he came across any Humans was a different matter.

Before they came to the little village at the bottom of the mountains, they had been searching the south. There weren't many Humans left down there now. The few that were left were becoming increasingly harder to find, which was why they had travelled this way in the first place.

Taredd didn't care where Arun was going. If he was heading back down south, then good luck to him. It wasn't going to be easy for either of them anyway. So north or south, they both stood the same chance in winning the bet.

It didn't take long for Taredd to reach the beginning of the pass that would take him through the mountains.

It should only take him a couple of days to reach the other side of the mountains from here. Taredd planned on walking through the night as well, so he could save time instead of wasting it.

Being a Demon had many perks, being able to see clearly in the dark was definitely one of the best. That, along with being able to regulate his body temperature, meant it was going to be more like a walk in the park instead of a freezing cold mountain pass.

"Are you following me?"

Taredd jumped at the sound of Arun's voice behind him.

"What the fuck are you doing here?" Taredd asked him. "I thought you had gone south again."

"I was thinking about it, but then I thought I would try my luck in the north instead," Arun said. "I take it you thought the same thing?"

"Yeah."

"Well, since we're heading in the same direction," Arun said. "We might as well walk together."

"What? Then split up on the other side of the mountains?" Taredd asked.

"Might as well," Arun said. "Unless you think you're going to find any along the pass?"

Shrugging one shoulder, Taredd said: "Nah, I can't see any of the Humans hiding out in the mountains. It's far too cold and the weather too unpredictable for them."

"True," Arun agreed. "So, how about it? Start the bet when we've reached the other side?"

"Okay then. We'll start the bet on the other side,"

Taredd agreed.

"Let's get going then," Arun said.

"What's the rush?" Taredd asked.

Not that he wanted to drag this bet out longer than needed, but Arun seemed extremely eager to get going... even more so than usual.

Looking up at the sky, Arun said: "I don't think the weather is going to hold out. There's a storm brewing, and when it hits, it's going to hit hard."

Taredd looked at the sky and had to agree. The weather was definitely changing, and not for the better.

"I was planning on traveling through the night," Taredd said. "It should only take us a couple of days to get there if we don't have to stop for the night, but looking at that sky, we might not have a choice in the matter."

"Yeah, I know, but hopefully we'll be able to cover some distance before we're forced to stop. Do you think we should tell Dain where we're heading?" Arun asked.

"No, he can find us easily enough on his own. Plus, I'm not going back to tell him, are you?" Taredd asked.

"It's fine by me," Arun agreed. "I'm certainly not going back for him."

"Good," Taredd said. "Because that would just be wasting even more time than we already are."

"How are we wasting time?" Arun asked.

"Because this bet is a waste of time," Taredd told him. "It would go a lot faster if we were all working together, and you know it would."

"I still don't think we're wasting time," Arun told him. "We're just having a bit of fun while we work, that's all. You need to have some fun every once in a while, otherwise you'll turn into a right miserable bastard."

"I'm not a miserable bastard," Taredd said.

"And I'm not saying you are. I'm just saying that you'll turn into one if you don't let your hair down…"

"My hair is down," he interrupted.

"…and have fun once in a while," Arun continued, not paying attention to Taredd's interruption. "At the end of the day, we are still working."

"Fine," he conceded. "Just don't take forever tracking one down."

"Don't worry, I won't. I plan on winning the bet, after all," Arun said confidently.

"We'll see," Taredd said, rolling his eyes.

"You really don't think I can do it, do you?" Arun asked.

"Oh, I know you can. Just not as quickly as I can," Taredd said smugly.

"Whatever," Arun said. "We'll soon see who's fastest."

"Yes, we will. And when that time comes, I look forward to taking all your money," Taredd said, smiling.

"I already know what I'm spending your money on, so I hope you're not too attached to it," Arun replied.

"I was about to say the same thing to you," Taredd laughed.

"How about you both shut up about it. You're giving

me a headache already."

They both spun round at the sound of Dain's voice.

"What the fuck are you doing here?" Arun asked him.

"I was bored waiting to see who wins, so I thought I would come along for the ride," he told them. "The thing I want to know, is why are you two together? I thought you would have gone separate ways. You know, it kind of defeats the purpose of the bet if you don't?"

"We're not working together," Arun said.

"Then what are you doing?" Dain asked.

"We're just traveling through the mountain pass together. Then we're going to start the bet when we split up on the other side," Taredd told him.

"Okay," he said, nodding his head. "That makes more sense. But why are you both going north?"

"I'm going north because we were heading in this direction anyway," Arun replied.

"And, I'm going north because I thought it was the best chance of finding a Human. We've already found most of the ones hiding in the south, so it was only logical to go this way," Taredd replied.

"Yeah, but you could have both taken different routes north, so why didn't you?" Dain asked.

"Basically, we bumped into each other at the beginning of the pass, so we thought we'd carry on this way together," Arun told him.

"Okay, makes sense now," Dain said finally.

"Oh, I'm so relieved it makes sense to you at last," Arun said sarcastically.

"I was only asking, there's no need to be such a dick about it," Dain said.

"Well, it's like explaining things to a child at times," Arun told him.

"I'm not a child. I'm older than you for fuck sake," Dain said.

"I didn't say you were a child. I said it's like explaining everything to a child," Arun pointed out. "There is a big difference between the two."

"Both of you, shut the fuck up bitching at each other," Taredd snapped.

"Ooh, no need to get snappy," Dain told him. "I'm only fucking about with him."

"Well, stop it," Taredd said. "I can't be assed listening to it today."

"I think someone needs a holiday," Arun said to Dain.

"I don't need a fucking holiday. I just need you two to stop fucking bitching at each other for more than five fucking minutes," he told them. "Is that too much to ask?"

"We're not always bitching at each other," Arun said.

"No, sometimes we're bitching at you," Dain added, making them both laugh.

"I swear you two are trying my patience today," Taredd said, scowling at them.

"I'm pretty sure we try your patience every day," Dain said.

Taredd rubbed his forehead. He was starting to get a headache from these two. He was beginning to wonder why he'd come this way in the first place.

Why couldn't he have just gone south? Or even east or west? But no, he had to pick the same bloody direction as Arun, and Dain just had to catch up with them.

Knowing his luck, even if Taredd had picked a different direction, he would have still ended up with the pair of them. So, he might as well make the best of it.

Taredd couldn't wait until they reached the other side of the mountain and split up. He was looking forward to a bit of peace and quiet away from them both, even if it was just for a little while. He only hoped they didn't keep bumping into each other after they split up as well.

The only problem was, it would take them a few days before they reached the other side and could at last go their own way. Until then, Taredd would be forced to put up with them.

This is going to be a long fucking journey. He thought to himself.

CHAPTER FOUR

Natalia

"Everyone else is packed up and ready to go," Amberly said as she walked over to Natalia.

"Good. We'll get going in just a minute. I have a couple more bits to finish putting away first," Natalia told her.

Not everything they've been using in the bunker was coming with them. Wherever they stayed, the items that were already there they left for other groups to use.

Some of the other groups weren't as lucky as them, they didn't have a lot of their own belonging, like blankets and cooking equipment. So, it was vitally important that those items were available for them to use. That's if they made it to one of the bunkers in the first place.

"Okay, I'll let the others know," Amberly said.

"Thanks."

"No problem."

Natalia quickly finished putting away all the items they had used and packed the last of her personal belongings into her satchel, then she joined the others in the main room.

"Ready to leave?" she asked as she walked in.

"More than ready," Donovan said.

"I still think we should wait for the others. They might make it back okay," Bella said.

"You know the rules, Bella. If you want to wait, then you can, but we are leaving now," Natalia told her.

"You'll be waiting on your own, unless someone else is going to volunteer to wait with you?" Amberly asked, as she looked around at the group.

Not one person stepped forward or piped up and said that they were willing to stay behind.

"See? Everyone else is leaving, so if you want to stay behind, you'll be doing it alone," Natalia said. "If not, then pick up your shit, because we're leaving now."

Bella looked around at everyone in the room, silently begging them to stay with her. When nobody did, she picked up her satchel and said: "Fine." before storming out the door and up the stairs to the exit.

Natalia, Amberly, and Donovan watched as the rest of the group followed Bella out of the bunker. They hung back to make sure that nobody was left behind and the bunker was left in the same condition they'd found it in. It also gave them a chance to talk about the others without being overheard.

"She'll be okay," Amberly said. "Just give her some time."

"I know," Natalia said.

"It's only because they were together before they

joined us," Donovan said.

"I heard they did things differently in their previous group," Amberly said.

"That may be the case, but this is the rule here. Everyone knows that if you're not back from a run before we move on to the next place, then you're left behind. It's the only way we can assure everyone else's safety," Natalia said.

"You don't have to tell us, we already know the rules," Amberly reminded her.

"Yeah, I know you do. It's just frustrating when people join us, but then don't want to abide by the rules we set out. It's not as if any of them have to stay with us," Natalia said, shaking her head. "They are more than welcome to leave at any point."

"Don't worry yourself over it too much. Those people don't know a good thing when they see it," Donovan said. "And tough shit if they don't like the rules. Like you said, they knew the rules when they joined us, if they don't like them, then they are more than welcome to just fuck off."

"Donovan!" Amberly said sternly.

"What?" he said innocently.

"That's not a very nice thing to say," Amberly told him.

"I don't give a shit, it's the truth."

"It doesn't matter if it's the truth, there's still no need to say it like that," Amberly said. "Tell him, Natalia. He should be nicer."

"To be honest, Amberly, I'm starting to feel the same way."

"Really?" They asked in unison.

"Well, yeah. It's the same argument every time someone from a previous group doesn't return, and I'm tired of being the bad guy when I refuse to either wait for them to return, or to go looking for them." Natalia rubbed her head. "Sometimes I wish it was just the three of us. It would be so much easier that way."

"Yeah, but it wouldn't be easier when it comes to scavenging."

"Why wouldn't it?" she asked. "We go out in twos anyway so the only difference I see, is the fact there would only be one person left looking after the camp while the others are gone."

"Yeah, I suppose so," Amberly agreed.

"So why don't we?" Donovan asked.

"Because we have a responsibility to the others in the group. I know not everyone causes as much hassle as Bella, so it's not fair to just abandon them," Natalia said. "To be honest, I don't think they would last very long without us either."

"Why is that our problem?" Donovan asked.

"Because it would be like handing them over to the monsters. At least, some of them anyway," Natalia told him.

"I wouldn't mind handing Bella over to the monsters," Donovan said.

"Donovan!" Natalia and Amberly both snapped.

"What?" he said innocently. "You can't say she isn't fucking annoying. Constantly whining all the time and bitching about everyone."

"Are you sure?" Natalia asked. "Because I've not

heard her bitching about anyone."

"Me neither," Amberly added.

"Well, yeah. She's not exactly quiet about it," Donovan said.

"Who does she bitch about?" Natalia asked him.

"Everyone," he said, shrugging his shoulders. "But mostly you two."

"Why us?" Amberly asked. "We haven't done anything."

"I know you haven't, and so does everyone else," Donovan said. "But that doesn't stop her from finding something to bitch about. Mostly it because she thinks she could do a better job at leading the group."

"I don't lead the group," Amberly pointed out.

"I know, but you're Natalia's best friend," he told her.

"So are you," Natalia said.

"Don't worry," Donovan said. "She likes to bitch about me too. She seems to think the three of us have special treatment over everyone else."

"That's not true," Natalia said. "Everyone is treated the same, including us."

"I know," he said. "And so does everyone else."

"Do you know what? I really don't give a shit," Natalia said. "If she wants to bitch about me, then so be it. I'm not interested in making friends with her. I'm more concerned about keeping everyone safe."

Making friends had never been her priority, keeping everyone safe was. If that meant pissing off a few people along the way, then so be it.

"Anyway," Natalia said, changing the subject.

"Let's not keep everyone waiting any longer."

"Yeah, let's go," Amberly said.

"Okay," Donovan said, following behind them as they headed up the stairs. "But just so you know, I'm happy to dump the others and go our separate way anytime you want. Just say the word, and we're off."

Natalia smiled. No matter what, she could always count on Donovan and Amberly. She didn't lie about wanting it to be just the three of them, she was sick and tired of being the one in charge all the time. She didn't even know how she ended up being the one in charge in the first place. She certainly never wanted the responsibility that came with it.

Donovan and Amberly helped out as much as they could, but there was only so much they could do without having to come to Natalia, looking for her to lead them. Even if she did hand over the job to one of them, they would still go to her anyway.

"What took you so long?" Bella snapped at them when they stepped outside. "Anything could have happened to us while we stood here waiting for you three."

Natalia looked at the rest of them as they stood waiting. They all looked fed up and about ready to throttle Bella. Natalia had to admit, Bella did seem to have that effect on everyone... herself included.

"We were just discussing which direction we should take."

"It took you that long to decide that?" Bella asked incredulously. "I thought you decided already last night. We're going north, aren't we?"

"Yes, we're heading north, but there are many different routes to take. We were deciding which one was going to be the best," Natalia told her.

"I take it you've finally come to a conclusion?"

"Yes."

"Well, can we get going now? Or have you decided to give the others a chance to get back first?"

Natalia rubbed her forehead with the tips of her fingers. "I'm not going through this with you again, Bella."

"Just shut the fuck up with that already," Donovan snapped. "It's not happening. If you want to stay, then stay. If not, keep your fucking mouth shut."

The look on Bella's face was comical. She looked as if Donovan had slapped her instead of just shouted at her. Natalia would have laughed if he hadn't shouted so loudly while they stood out in the open.

So instead, she whacked him across the arm and said "Not so loud, Donovan. You're gonna give away our location if any of the monsters are within hearing distance, and you know how far some of them can hear."

"Oh, here she goes again" Bella rolled her eyes. "Call them by name. Yes, they are all monsters, but ya know, you can call them Demons, Shifters, or Fae."

"I know they're not all the same, but it's easier to call them all monsters because it could be any, or all, of them that hear us. So, yes, they are monsters," Natalia said.

"Whatever. You just sound stupid calling them that," Bella said smugly.

"Just shut it, Bella," Donovan said.

"Please, shut up Bella," Amberly added.

She finally got the hint that nobody else shared her views, as one by one they each told her to shut up in one form or another.

"Fine!" she snapped. "I won't say another word."

Thank fuck for that, Natalia thought.

She didn't dare say it aloud, even though she really wanted to, just in case it started off another argument.

"Lead the way, Natalia," Donovan said, holding his arm out for her to take the lead.

Taking a deep breath, she lifted her satchel onto her shoulder and said "Let's go then."

Without actually deciding with Donovan and Amberly on which direction they were going to take, Natalia just started walking straight towards the mountains. It might not be the safest route to take, but it was the shortest.

Natalia didn't know what they were going to find on the other side of the mountain, but it couldn't be much worse than what they faced this side.

"Ignore Bella. Nobody else thinks the same way as her," Amberly said, as she walked along beside Natalia.

"I know they don't," Natalia told her.

"From the sounds of it, everyone is sick and tired of listening to her," Amberly said, then quietly added: "I'm going to speak to some of the others to find out what she's been saying about us."

"Don't bother, it doesn't matter," Natalia said truthfully.

"I know it doesn't. I just want to know, that's all," Amberly said.

"I don't think you do," Natalia told her. "Whatever she's been saying, I don't think you'll like it. It's more than likely going to upset you even more than you are now."

"I'm not upset," Amberly said adamantly.

"You're not?" Natalia asked, looking at her with a raised eyebrow.

"No, I'm pissed off," she said angrily. "How dare she say anything bad about us, especially you."

"Why *especially me*?"

"Because of everything you've done for us all. She has no right bitching about you when you've done nothing but make everyone feel welcome and safe," Amberly's hands were balled into fists as she spoke.

Natalia couldn't fault Amberly's reasoning, but she still didn't think it was a good idea. Natalia didn't know what had been said about them, but she knew whatever it was, Amberly would end up getting more upset.

"Please don't bother on my account," Natalia told her. "She's more than welcome to say whatever the fuck she wants. I really don't care."

Amberly looked over at Natalia to see if she meant what she said, which she did, before saying: "Okay, I won't."

At the end of the day, Bella's opinion of her didn't matter. As long as everyone in the group stayed safe, Bella could say whatever the fuck she wanted about Natalia. That's all that really mattered nowadays anyway.

Amberly didn't say another word about the matter. Instead, she walked quietly by Natalia's side for the rest of the day.

CHAPTER FIVE

Taredd

"Is it just me, or does this pass get longer each time we come through here," Dain asked.

"It's just you," Arun told him.

"It probably feels longer because you have usually given up walking with us by now. Generally, you shift into a bird or something, and have abandoned us by this point," Taredd said.

"I don't do that, do I?" Dain asked, looking at Arun.

"Yep, Taredd's right," Arun agreed. "Normally you meet us on the other side."

"Yeah, I suppose that does sound like something I'd do," Dain said, smirking.

Taredd had to admit, he was surprised Dain was still with them. Normally he'd long since left them by the time they reached this point, preferring to take to the sky and meet them on the other side.

Taredd hoped this wasn't the start of Dain's complaining though, because they still had a couple of days travel. That was if they didn't stop at night. The last thing Taredd wanted was to spend the whole time listening to Dain complain about it every step of the way.

"We've still got quite a way to go yet, so why don't you just fly on ahead and meet us there like normal?" Taredd asked him.

"What? And miss all this fun? I don't think so," Dain said, smiling.

"You call this fun?" Arun asked. "If I had your abilities, I would have done that at the start of day one. I've had enough of wearing wet clothes already."

"And you thought I was going to be the one moaning, didn't you?" Dain asked Taredd.

"You've got magic," Taredd said. "Use it to dry your clothes."

"What do you think I have been doing?" Arun snapped. "It doesn't matter how many times I dry my clothing, within minutes it's soaked through again."

"I seriously wonder why I stick around with you two," Taredd said, shaking his head at them. "One, if not both, of you are always fucking moaning about something. In fact, I don't think we've gone a single day without one of you finding something to bitch about."

"That's not true," Arun said.

"Yeah," Dain agreed. "There was one day the other week were neither of us bitched about anything. I remember it well because it was such a boring day."

"It was, wasn't it." Arun laughed.

"Where the hell was I then, because I don't remember any day in the last century where you two haven't bitched," Taredd told them.

"Yeah... I don't think you were with us that day,"

Dain said.

"Hadn't he gone ahead of us to scout the area where the last group of Humans we were hunting had been spotted?" Arun asked.

"I think he might have done," Dain said.

"So, the one day I could have had peace and quiet around you, I was off scouting ahead?" Taredd asked.

"Yeah, I'm sure that was the same day," Dain said.

Sounds about right. Taredd thought before he said: "To be honest, that doesn't surprise me. I bet you're the same every time I scout ahead, aren't you?"

"I don't know about every time," Arun said.

"But most times," Dain admitted, grinning from ear to ear.

"You're a dick," Taredd told him.

"Yeah, I know, I got a pretty big dick," Dain said smugly.

"I didn't say that," Taredd said.

Smiling, Dain said: "You didn't have to."

"Just change into a bird or something and fuck off already," Taredd told him.

"Can't do that, you'd miss me too much," Dain said.

"I fucking wouldn't," he said adamantly.

"Oh, you would," Dain said, grinning. "You may not admit it, but I know you love having me around."

"Yeah, like I love stabbing hot pokers into my eyes," Taredd said sarcastically.

"There's no need to be like that," Arun said. "It's not that bad having Dain around."

"You like stabbing hot pokers in your eyes?" Dain asked. Shaking his head, he added "You Demons are a really weird bunch of fuckers. I don't see how anyone would love to do something like that."

"Oh, for fuck sake," Taredd said, rubbing his forehead.

"What's wrong now?" Dain asked.

Slapping him around the head, Arun told him: "You're giving him a headache with your stupidity."

"I'm only messing with him," Dain said, laughing. "I know he doesn't like sticking hot pokers in his eyes."

"He's not giving me a headache," Taredd said. "Because I already have one."

"Do you want me to use my magic to get rid of the pain?" Arun offered.

"No, thank you. Can we just walk in silence for a while, please?" Taredd asked them both.

"Yeah, of course," Arun said.

"I suppose," Dain pouted.

"Thank you," Taredd said.

Taredd didn't have a headache, but if it meant he could have a bit of peace and quiet, then he was more than happy to lie and tell them he did. He didn't even feel guilty about it either. It wasn't as if they've never lied to him, or each other, if it suited them in the past.

From the look of it, they weren't going to be walking for much longer today. While they had been bickering, the weather had been slowly deteriorating. Taredd guessed they had another hour or so, before it was going to be too difficult to see through the snowstorm, that had been building up.

"We're going to have to look for shelter soon," Arun said, reading Taredd's mind.

"I know," he agreed.

"It's getting too fucking cold for me. I need to shift into something with a little more fur," Dain told them.

Taredd didn't blame him. Dain couldn't regulate his body temperature as well as Taredd and Arun could. The only way for Dain to stay warm in the rapidly plummeting temperatures, was to either put on more layers, or shift into an animal with fur.

"No problem," Arun said.

Dain didn't say another word. One moment he was stood in his Human form, then within a blink of an eye a dark grey wolf stood in his place.

"Better?" Taredd asked as he looked down at the wolf.

Dain nodded his head to let them know he was ready, then they started walking again. This time, they kept a look out for a place they could take shelter from the storm. As much as Taredd wanted to get this bet over and done with so they could get back to normality, he wasn't willing to travel when he couldn't see where he was going.

Pointing towards a black shadow in the snow, Arun shouted over the noise of the wind as it picked up speed. "I see a place over there."

"Okay," Taredd shouted back.

It didn't take long for them to reach the cave. Dain ran off ahead and was already waiting for them when they reach it.

Sat in his Human form, Dain said as they walked in. "I've checked the cave. There's no animals taking shelter here."

"Good," Taredd said.

The last thing they wanted to do was to disturb any wildlife in the area.

"Now that you're here," Dain said to Arun. "Do you mind using your magic to start a fire? I'm fucking freezing my ass off here."

"Sure," Arun nodded as he walked over to where Dain was sitting.

Within seconds, Arun had a fire roaring in front of Dain.

"Thanks a bunch," Dain said as he stretched his arms out towards the flames.

"How long do you think this storm is going to last?" Taredd asked.

"I don't know. It could be as little as a few hours, or it could last for days," Arun said.

"Wonderful," Taredd said.

The last thing he wanted, was to be stuck in a cave for days with Arun and Dain.

"At least Arun can magic us up some grub," Dain said, looking on the bright side.

"I never said I was going to feed you as well as keep you warm," Arun told him.

"You can't let me starve," Dain whined. "I'm a growing lad, I need plenty of food."

"Don't start. I'm not in the mood to listen to either of you right now. Arun, stop tormenting Dain, you know you're going to sort out some food for all of us," Taredd said. "And Dain... just shut the fuck up."

"That's it?" Dain asked.

"Yeah, that's it. Just shut the fuck up for a while,

okay?" Taredd said.

"Okay then," Dain said, dragging out the words before looking at Arun and saying "Someone definitely got up on the wrong side of the bed this morning."

"I wasn't in bed this morning," Taredd told him. "In fact, I haven't been in bed for days."

"Yeah, I know. Neither have I," Dain replied.

"None of us have," Arun added.

Sighing, Taredd said: "I know. So, how about we have something to eat, then get some well-deserved sleep while the storm passes?"

"Sounds good to me," Arun said.

"Yeah, me too," Dain agreed.

"What do you both want to eat?" Arun asked them.

"To be honest, I don't really care as long as it's food," Taredd told him.

Which was true, he didn't care what he ate as long as he had something. Taredd was more interested in finally getting some sleep. As long as Arun and Dain could shut up for long enough, that is. Moving over to the side of the cave, he sat down and leaned against the wall. Closing his eyes, he listened as the other two talked while Arun used his magic to manifest some food.

"Here you go, Taredd," Arun said after a couple of minutes. "Sorry if I woke you."

"Thanks," he said, taking the offered plate. "You didn't wake me because I wasn't asleep, just resting my eyes."

"It sure looked like you were sleeping from where

I'm sitting," Dain said.

"Well, I wasn't," he snapped.

"Okay, no need to get snappy with me," Dain said, holding his hands up.

"Sorry, I'm just tired, that's all," Taredd apologized.

"I know man, we all are," Dain said.

"Get that down ya, then you can get some sleep," Arun said, pointing to the food.

"Yeah, I'm going to," he said.

Taredd tucked in to the food as Arun took a seat across from Dain by the fire. They needed the heat more than he did. Arun had to rest his magic just as much as his body, so Taredd was more than happy to sit further away from the flames.

Dain was the first to finish eating, which was no surprise. Taredd was positive Dain didn't bother chewing his food before swallowing, just shovelled it in and swallowed it whole. It was the only explanation Taredd could come up with as to how Dain could eat so fast.

Taredd and Arun liked to take their time eating, savouring their food. Many times, Dain had complained, saying that they took too long, but neither of them cared. They would rather take their time and enjoy their meal.

Within minutes of Dain finishing his meal, he was snoring his head off, sprawled out next to the fire.

"I don't know how the fuck he does that," Arun said.

"Me neither," Taredd admitted.

"I wish I could fall asleep as easily as he does," Arun said.

"You and me both," Taredd agreed.

It didn't matter where they were, Dain always managed to fall asleep within seconds of closing his eyes. It took Taredd ages to switch his brain off so he could sleep. Tonight however, he didn't think that was going to be a problem.

"It's going to take me ages now, his snoring is going to keep me awake," Arun moaned.

Normally it would play a part in keeping Taredd awake as well, but he was so tired he didn't think anything was going to disturb him tonight. Not the cold. Not the solid rock. And certainly not Dain and his snoring.

CHAPTER SIX

Natalia

"Why have you brought us this way?" Bella demanded. "You shouldn't have worried about the monsters killing us." She used her fingers to make air quotes when she said 'monsters', which Natalia decided to ignore. "No, you're going to make us freeze to death instead."

"Don't be so melodramatic, Bella. None of us are going to freeze to death," Donovan told her.

"Not all of us, no, because I for one am not going in there." She folded her arms in front of her chest.

Natalia had known that Bella was going to cause problems when she decided to take this route. That's one of the reasons why she hadn't said anything before they arrived at the beginning of the mountain pass. She would have kept it secret for even longer if she could have, but unfortunately, she couldn't hide it when it was right in front of them.

"I'm telling you, she's going to get us all killed," Bella said.

Finally reaching the end of her patience, Natalia turned to face Bella.

"I tell you what, you want to go your own way, then by all means... go. If not, then shut the fuck up. I've had enough of listening to you now." Looking around at everyone else in the group, she added: "And that goes for the rest of you as well. If you don't want to be here, then fuck off, because no one is forcing you to stay. Either way, I don't care, I'm taking this route north. If you want to come with me, then you best be ready to go because I'm leaving now."

Without saying another word... or even looking at any of them... Natalia started walking. She didn't care one way or another if they joined her because she was more than happy to make the journey on her own.

"I'm with you, always," Amberly said, coming up alongside her.

"Me too," Donovan said as he joined them.

Smiling, Natalia said "I thought you two might."

"You best believe it, because you're not getting rid of us that easily," Donovan said, wrapping his arm around her shoulders.

"We couldn't lose you if we tried," Amberly said.

"And it's not like we haven't tried," Natalia said playfully.

"Now you see, I know you're only kidding," he said smugly. "You two would be lost without me."

"Hah, I think you've got that the wrong way around," Natalia told him.

"I'm with Natalia, it's definitely you who needs us," Amberly agreed. "Half the time you don't know which way is north, even when we're heading in that direction."

"If you're talking about yesterday, that was just a joke," he said. "I knew that was east, I was just testing that you two knew it."

Natalia and Amberly shared a look, before bursting out laughing.

"I'm telling you the truth," he said.

"Yeah, whatever you need to tell yourself," Natalia said.

"Looks like everyone except Bella is coming with us." Amberly looked back at the group. "Do you think one of us should go back for her?"

"My answer would be no, let her fend for herself," Donovan said.

"We can't do that," Amberly said.

"Why the hell not?" he asked. "It'll be a lot quieter without her."

"Yeah, that may be, but she wouldn't last two minutes out there on her own, and you know it," Amberly told him.

As much as Natalia hated to admit it, Amberly was right. It wasn't safe for any of them to be alone, especially someone like Bella. She could barely cook a meal and that was only if somebody else started a fire for her, because she couldn't start one on her own. So, there was no way she would last very long on her own.

"Amberly's right, someone has to go back for her," Natalia said.

"Well, I'm not," Donovan was adamant.

"I know you're not," Natalia said. "I'm going back for her, and I'm going on my own."

"You can't go alone, Natalia. At least take someone

else with you," Amberly said.

"No, I'm not going to risk anyone else for her," Natalia said.

"Don't go at all," Donovan told her. "Just leave her to fend for herself."

"I can't do that either," Natalia told him.

"Why?" Amberly asked.

"You know why," Natalia said.

Natalia could see Amberly was getting upset about it, but there was no other choice. Natalia could never live with herself if something happened to Bella and she didn't do anything to prevent it.

"Fine," Donovan sighed. "I'll come with you."

"No, you won't," Natalia told him. "I need you and Amberly to make sure everyone else makes it safely through the pass."

"I can do that on my own," Amberly said. "Take Donovan with you."

"No. I've made my mind up. I want you two to look after the rest of the group." Taking Amberly's hands in hers, she added: "I will be okay, I promise."

"But..."

"No buts, Amberly," she said sternly. "I need to do this, and I need you two looking after the rest of the group."

Natalia could see the worry in Amberly's eyes, but there wasn't anything she could do about it. At the end of the day, it was Natalia's responsibility to make sure everybody in the group was safe.

Softening her voice, she said: "I promise I'll be okay, and I'll catch up with you before you know it."

"You best do," Amberly told her. "If you don't, I'll find you and beat the shit out of you."

Natalia laughed. "You couldn't hurt a fly, let alone beat the shit out of me."

"It's not funny, Natalia," Amberly said. "I'm serious, you best catch up with us."

"Amberly may not be able to beat the shit out of you, but I certainly can," Donovan told her. "So, you best do as she says."

"I will, I promise," she said again.

Natalia didn't know how many times she was going to have to promise them before they believed her, but she was definitely coming back. There was no way in hell Natalia was going to let Bella keep her away from Amberly and Donovan for too long. So, the faster she left, the faster she was going to be able to catch up with them again.

"Fine, but be as quick as you can," Amberly told her.

"And if you can't find her quickly enough, then just leave her," Donovan said. "Because she obviously wants to go her own way."

"I'll give it a day," Natalia said. "If I can't find her in that time, then I'll turn around and come find you. How's that sound?"

"I would be happier if it was just half a day," Amberly said.

"You know I can't do that," Natalia said, shaking her head. "I have to give it at least a day."

"Okay, one day, but no longer than that," Amberly said sternly.

Natalia stuck out her tongue. "Yes, mum."

"Well, what are you waiting for?" Donovan said. "Stop walking further along the pass with us and head back now before she gets too much of a head start on you."

Amberly stopped walking. "He's right. You could have caught up with her in the time that's passed since we noticed she wasn't with us."

"I know," Natalia said. "But I didn't want to turn back until I knew you two were happy to carry on without me."

"Well, we're not happy," Amberly said. "But since we can't change your mind, we'd rather you head back as soon as possible, so you can catch back up to us quicker."

"Okay," Natalia said. "I'm going."

Natalia hugged Amberly and then Donovan.

"Stay safe," Donovan whispered in her ear.

"I will," she whispered back before letting go.

"Right," she said. "Stick together, and when you reach the other side, find somewhere safe to stay until I catch up with you. If I'm not back in a week, move on without me."

"No," they said in unison.

"Yes," she countered. "You know the rules. You can't ignore them because it's me."

"Yes, we can," Amberly said.

"No, you can't," Natalia said. "We can't have one rule for one and another for everyone else."

"She's right, Amberly," Donovan said. "As much as I hate to agree with her, she's right."

"Fine," Amberly gave in. "But you best be back in time."

"I will," Natalia told her. "Right, I best get going. Don't forget, one week."

"We will," Donovan assured her.

"Good. Now get going. It'll be dark before too long," Natalia told them.

"See you soon, Natalia," Amberly said.

"Take care," Donovan said as he hooked his arm with Amberly's and walked away.

Natalia watched as they headed further along the pass. When they walked around a bend and vanished from view, she took a deep breath and turned back around.

She wasn't looking forward to searching for Bella, especially not on her own. But she couldn't leave her behind, and she refused to risk anyone else's life, so she had no choice. Natalia had to do this, and she had to do it alone.

Fingers crossed I find her soon, Natalia thought as she retraced her steps.

If not, then she would have no choice but to give up and join up again with the rest of the group. That wasn't going to happen until the last possible minute though.

Natalia guessed she had a couple more hours of daylight to search for her, then she needed to find someplace safe to spend the night. If Natalia hasn't found her by then, she'll restart the search first thing in the morning and spend the whole day looking before following after the others.

Bella best not have gone too far.

She didn't want to spend too long away from the rest of the group. Not only that, but the weather over the mountain was getting worse by the minute. Natalia didn't think it was going to be safe to travel through the pass if she left it too much longer.

With that thought in mind, Natalia picked up the pace. If she could find Bella before nightfall, then they could be back on the pass no later than mid-morning tomorrow.

The rest of the group would still be on the pass at that point, so if they were quick enough, they could catch up before they reached the other side. That would be the best scenario, but Natalia had a feeling it wasn't going to be so easy. Especially if she had to convince Bella to go with her.

Natalia didn't yet know what she was going to do if Bella still refused to go with them by the time she found her. If that was going to be the case, then Natalia would have to travel the pass on her own, which wasn't the wisest idea but what else could she do.

Either way, Natalia needed to find Bella to make sure she was okay.

CHAPTER SEVEN

Taredd

Taredd was more than ready to leave the cave by the time the storm passed. It was bad enough that Dain and Arun were still dead set on wasting time with this stupid bet, but being stuck in the cave for days on end as well had Taredd inching to get it over and done with.

He wanted them to get back to what they did best. Hunting the Humans as a group. It was the most efficient way to rid the world of their kind.

"If you two don't hurry the fuck up, I'm leaving without you," Taredd told them.

Taredd didn't know how the fuck it could take them so long to get ready to leave when they didn't have anything to take with them. As soon as he woke up, Taredd was ready to leave.

"Hold ya horses. We're nearly ready," Dain said.

"I seriously don't understand what takes you both so long to get ready, it's not as if you're packing anything to take with you," Taredd told them.

"Are we not allowed to have something to eat before we go?" Arun asked.

"It doesn't take half the day to eat breakfast," Taredd pointed out.

"For someone who hasn't slept in a bed, it's like he got out the wrong side again," Dain said around a mouth full of food.

"That's probably why he's in such a foul mood. He's too used to the comforts of a soft mattress," Arun said.

"That's not it," Taredd told them.

"What is it then?" Arun asked.

"I just want to get going," Taredd said. "We've already spent more than enough time here."

"Are you getting withdrawals?" Dain asked him.

"Withdrawals from what?" he asked, confused.

"Hunting? Humans? I don't know, you tell us what it might be," Dain said, shrugging his shoulders.

"Oh, for fuck sake," Taredd said. "I'm not going through withdrawal for anything."

"Are you sure?" Dain asked.

"Yes, of course I'm sure," he said adamantly.

"How would you know if you were going through withdrawal or not?" Dain asked him.

"Because I would just know, okay?" he said.

Dain turned to Arun and said "I think he's delusional as well."

"If the look on his face is anything to go on, he's close to beating the shit out of you," Arun told him.

Dain turned back to Taredd. He could imagine that steam was billowing out of his ears from Dain's reaction.

"I think you've pissed him off this time," Arun said.

"He knows I'm only fucking with him," Dain said.

"You know I'm only playing with you, don't ya Taredd?"

"Can you not give up being an ass for just one day?" Taredd asked him.

"Yeah, I can," Dain said.

"Then please, make it today," Taredd said.

"Okay, fine. I'll be on my best behaviour for today," Dain agreed. "But for twenty-four hours only."

"I'll take it," Taredd told him.

"Well, I suppose we best get going then, if you're both ready?" Arun asked.

Taredd scowled at them. He'd been trying to get them to leave for hours. If he'd known all it would take for them to get their asses into gear was for him to show how pissed off he was getting, then he would have done that hours ago.

"Yeah, I'm ready to go now," Dain said.

"About fucking time." Taredd threw his hands up in the air. "That's it, this is the last time I'm waiting for you two. From now on, if you're not ready when I am, then I'm leaving without you."

"To be honest, I'm surprised you haven't left us behind before now," Arun said as he followed Taredd out of the cave, Dain hot on his heels.

"The thought has crossed my mind many times in the past," Taredd told him.

"Then why haven't you?" Arun asked.

"Because we're a team. You don't leave members of your team behind, no matter how annoying they are," he said, pointedly staring in Dain's direction.

"Hey, I'm not the only one that annoys you," he said.

"Arun is just as bad as me."

Taredd couldn't stop the laugh that burst out of him.

"I'm not as bad as you," Arun said, insulted.

"Yes, you are," Dain said.

"I have to agree with Arun," Taredd said. "He isn't as bad as you."

"See? I told you," Arun said smugly. "I don't know anyone that is more annoying than you are, and I know a lot of annoying people."

"If that's how you both feel, then I should just leave," Dain said. "You obviously don't like having me around, so why the fuck am I still here?"

"That's not true. Just because you're the most annoying creature to roam the planet," Arun said. "Doesn't mean we don't like having you around."

"We just want you to have a day off from being a dick head every once in a while," Taredd said.

"How often is 'once in a while'?" Dain asked.

"At least once a week," Arun said.

"More if you can," Taredd added.

"I see. It's like that, is it?" Dain said.

"Yeah, it's like that," Taredd said, nodding his head.

"Fine," Dain said. "I promise to have at least one day a week off from being a dick."

"Great," Taredd said.

"Fantastic," Arun added.

"Now, shall we pick up the pace?" Taredd asked.

"Lead the way," Arun replied.

Dain didn't say a word. Instead, he grunted his agreement. Taredd wasn't stupid, he knew Dain was hurt by what they just told him, but he didn't seem to get the hint any other way.

Taredd wasn't bothered about them having a laugh, but every single day was taking the piss a little. Even he like to have a laugh, but all the time? No. Sometimes it was nice to have a peaceful day without anyone fucking about, or being a complete dick like Dain was, more often than not.

Dain was a great friend, and Taredd never wanted to lose that friendship. He just wanted Dain to take life more seriously at times. Was that too much to ask? Taredd didn't think it was.

They managed to cover a far bit of distance as they all walked in silence, all of them lost in their own thoughts. Occasionally they stopped for something to eat, but other than that they continued traipsing through the snow.

Taredd was amused when neither of them wanted to stop for the night, especially after all the shit they gave him about not being used to sleeping on anything other than a soft mattress, so they carried on walking through the night. Luckily enough they could all go several days without needing to rest.

They managed to make it nearly two days before Dain finally asked that dreaded question.

"Are we there yet?" he asked.

Here we go, Taredd thought.

He knew it wouldn't be too much longer before Dain had started with the 'are we there yet' question. To be honest, Taredd was surprised it took him this long. He'd been expecting it since they left the cave.

"Nearly," Taredd and Arun said in unison.

"I'm in need of a stiff drink," Dain said.

"I second that," Arun said.

"I third that," Taredd added.

"Are you sure we're not there yet?" Dain asked.

"Is there still snow surrounding us?" Taredd asked instead.

"Well, yeah," Dain said.

"Then we're not fucking there yet," Taredd told him. "So, stop asking before I push you off the next cliff we come across."

"I don't think we're going to come across any more cliffs," Arun pointed out.

"I'm sure I can find one," he said.

They just couldn't help themselves, they just loved to annoy him, he was sure of it.

"I only asked twice," Dain pointed out.

"Well, I thought I'd tell you before we had to hear it like a broken record," Taredd told him.

"I don't do that," Dain said.

"Yeah, you do," Taredd said.

"I take it you think the same?" Dain asked Arun, who nodded in agreement. "Fine, I won't ask again."

"Good," Taredd said.

After a couple of minutes walking in silence, Dain asked: "Do you think we'll be there by nightfall?"

Taredd groaned. It was basically the same bloody question, just worded differently.

"Seriously?" Arun asked.

"What?" Dain asked.

"Taredd already told you it's not much further, so shut the fuck up about it." Arun shook his head. "You going on about it, makes it feel even further away."

"Fine, I just won't say another fucking word then, okay?" Dain snapped.

"Yes," Taredd replied.

"Thank the Goddess," Arun said, looking up at the sky. "He's finally going to shut up."

"I seriously don't know why I hang out with you two," Dain told them. "You can be right miserable bastards at times."

"You hang out with us because you would be bored otherwise," Arun told him.

"I'm sure I could find something else to pass the time," Dain said. "After all, there's plenty of females..."

"That you haven't had sex with?" Arun interrupted. "Because I don't think there is."

Punching Arun in the arm, Dain said: "I haven't slept with that many females."

Arun laughed. "Yeah right, and I haven't had that many hot meals."

"Maybe you could find something to pass the time," Taredd said. "But then you couldn't annoy us all the time, which we both know you secretly take great pleasure from."

"No, I don't," Dain said it as if he was hurt by the comment.

"Yeah, you do," Taredd said.

"Yes, you do," Arun agreed.

"Yeah, you're right. I do," Dain said, smiling.

Taredd shook his head.

"You're a dick head, you know that?" Arun asked.

"Just on Tuesdays," Dain laughed.

Dain was never going to change, he was never going to stop being an annoying twat, and they both knew it. But that was Dain for you, and it wouldn't be the same if he was any other way. Admittedly, it would be a lot more peaceful, but it wouldn't be half as much fun.

"Do you even know what day of the week it is?" Arun asked him.

"Nope." Dain said, shaking his head. "And I really couldn't give a shit either."

"Do you?" Taredd asked Arun.

"Hell no," Arun said. "But do I need to know? No, I don't. After all, that's a Human thing."

"Yeah, I know," Taredd said.

Why the Humans needed to name the days, he would never understand. Taredd didn't even care if it was night or day, summer or winter. It was all the same to him.

CHAPTER EIGHT

Natalia

Natalia searched for far longer than she planned to, but since the weather had made it too dangerous to travel along the pass, she had time to kill and she didn't want to kill it by sitting around doing fuck all. She might as well spend it trying to find Bella. Not that she was having any luck, but it was still better than doing nothing.

It was as if Bella had vanished into thin air. The only sign Natalia had seen of Bella after turning back for her, was at the entrance of the pass. After that Natalia hadn't come across any sign of her. Which was weird because Bella wasn't prone to covering her tracks.

In fact, out of everyone Natalia has ever known in her life, Bella was by far the easiest to find. This time though, there was nothing. Not even a random foot print in the mud or anything.

Natalia knew something wasn't right. Bella couldn't have just vanished, someone must have taken her, but after days of searching there was still no sign of her or anyone else having been in the area.

With nothing else to do, and completely out of ideas of where else to look, Natalia had to call it a day on the search. The others needed her more and they didn't need her to get herself caught by the monsters while searching for someone who obviously didn't want to be found. If she did get caught, Amberly and Donovan would never give up looking for her, even though it would be in vain. So, she needed to get back to them before they sent out a search party for her.

Even though she told them not to, if she didn't return, they would worry about her and then they would end up breaking the rules to find her. That was the last thing she wanted. She couldn't have one rule for everyone else and a separate one for herself, even if she was the leader of the group.

As it was, by the time the storm had cleared enough for her to attempt the pass, several days had gone by. She hoped the others made it through before the weather turned. If not, then she prayed that they were able to find shelter along the way.

Natalia finished packing her satchel and then headed for the pass. The weather still wasn't great, but at least it wasn't a complete whiteout over the mountains any more. When Natalia first attempted to join the others, she could barely see the mountains through a cloud of white. It wasn't clear blue skies this time around, but she could at least see the tops of the mountains, which was a vast improvement from last time. It meant that she would be able to see where she's going.

The last thing Natalia wanted... or needed... was to step in the wrong place as she tried to navigate the treacherous mountain pass. One wrong step could easily end her life. Natalia wasn't willing to die just yet, and especially not like that. She hadn't evaded the monsters all these years, just to die accidentally.

That would be rather ironic really, wouldn't it? Survive all these years, only to die by taking a wrong step. It sounded like something that would happen to her, but she wasn't going to let it happen if she could help it.

As she made her way further along the pass, Natalia regretted not finding something warmer to wear. The thin coat she was wearing barely kept her dry, and it did very little to keep her warm. The even thinner jumper she had on underneath wasn't much better.

"I need some more clothes," she mumbled to herself.

As soon as she met up with the others, she was going to put that at the top of her list of things to collect, along with food.

Her stomach grumbled for the thousandth time since she woke up. The meager amount of food she had on her when she left the others ran out days ago. Natalia had looked for some food while she was searching for Bella, but just like with Bella, there was no sign of any.

Natalia hoped that the others had managed to restock their supplies when they reached the other side. She hoped what little they did have with them had lasted them longer than it did her.

If they had found some, then it would mean she could have something to eat as soon as she caught up with them. With that thought in mind, Natalia picked up the pace. Even at a faster pace, it was going to be a couple of days before she even reached the other side. Then came the hard part of finding them.

Natalia didn't have a clue where they were staying. It could be a mile away from the mountains, or it could be twenty. It wasn't easy finding others of her kind anymore, which made her wonder how the monsters seemed to find them so easily.

Even after all these years nobody knew exactly what abilities or magic the monsters possessed. Those who got close enough to them to find out, never lived long enough to learn their secrets. And since the monsters weren't in a sharing kind of mood, there was no way to find out for sure.

Natalia had come across lots of books that featured the monsters, but as far as she could tell, none of it was real. It wasn't as if there were any books written by the monsters themselves. At least, none that Natalia had found and she had been looking for years. Even if there had been at some point in history, she wouldn't put it past the monsters to destroy all evidences of their existence.

Natalia would love to know their secret, she would love to know what powers they possessed, because she would happily use it against them if she could. Natalia wasn't an aggressive person by any means, but she would make an exception for the monsters, especially if it was a choice between her life and theirs.

If Amberly or Donovan's lives were on the line, then she would fight tooth and nail to keep them safe, even if it meant forfeiting her own life to save theirs. Natalia knew she should feel the same about the rest of the people in the group as well, but she didn't. As much as she tried to treat them all the same, Amberly and Donovan were more like her brother and sister, whereas the others she just couldn't see them the same way, no matter how much she wanted to.

Bella was just a completely different kettle of fish all together. At least Natalia liked the rest of the people in the group. But Bella? No, she couldn't stand the woman. Something about Bella grated on Natalia and she couldn't pinpoint what it was, but it had been that way ever since she joined the group. There was something just not quite right about her.

Nobody else in the group knew her feeling about Bella, she never mentioned it to anyone. Even Amberly and Donovan didn't know, because she didn't want her feeling to rub off on them or anyone else. At the end of the day, it might not be anything other than her simply not clicking with Bella.

As it was, Natalia had a feeling that not many of the others in the group liked Bella, if any of them. But if they found out what Natalia's view of her was, then it could have caused an even bigger rift between them all. It was probably all a moot subject now anyway, since it was unlikely any of them were ever going to see Bella again. So, there was no point in telling any of them now.

If they found out now, then they might even think that Natalia didn't bother looking for her as hard as she could have. So, it was in her best interest never to let anyone know, even Amberly and Donovan. None of it would matter if she didn't manage to find them anyway.

Natalia just hoped that she hadn't made a huge mistake in splitting up the group by going off on her own to look for Bella. It was possible that in doing so she had made it a permanent arrangement, but she knew the risk when she made the decision. She knew it could mean that she might never see any of them again.

Natalia couldn't let herself think that way though, she needed to stay positive for her own sanity, otherwise she might as well turn back now and not bother attempting to travel along the pass on her own. It was only the thought of seeing them again that kept her going as it was, if Natalia didn't have that then she would just give up and turn back.

It was also the thought of how much they relied on her, and the fact that she knew Amberly and Donovan would refuse to stop looking for her that spurred her on. Even if nobody else in the group would miss her, she knew Amberly and Donovan would.

Natalia knew without a doubt that they would search for her if she didn't catch up with them soon enough. She couldn't let them risk their lives trying to find her, so she had to push forward, she had to keep going until she found them.

So, here she was, traipsing through knee high snow as she navigates the treacherous mountain pass on her own. All in the hopes of reaching her friends... her family.

CHAPTER NINE

Taredd

It didn't take long for them to find the closest tavern once they left the pass. It was a bit further away from the pass than he would have liked, but it was better than nothing. After spending the last few days traveling, and one night in a cave, he was more than ready for a soft bed and a hell of a lot to drink.

They spent the rest of the day in the tavern, drinking and having a laugh. The room Taredd stayed in was much better than the last one, but it was nowhere close to his own bedroom back home. Taredd couldn't remember the last time he stepped foot inside his home. He had to admit, he was missing it and couldn't wait to go back.

The following morning, Taredd and Arun were up at the crack of dawn to start the bet. They split off to go their separate ways as soon as they left the tavern. Dain was still fast asleep when they left., Since he wasn't part of the bet, he could do whatever the hell he wanted.

Taredd didn't bother asking them where they were going to be. Arun would probably move around a lot as he hunted down his own Human anyway, and he knew that Dain could be found in any of the taverns... more than likely the same one they'd just left him in. It wasn't a problem though, because he could find them both easily enough when the time came, so he didn't bother to ask them.

Taredd decided to hang around and search the area closest to the mountains. His reasoning was that the Humans had to have a hideout somewhere close to the pass for when they travelled along it, kind of like a last pit stop before attempting the treacherous journey, or maybe even a safe place they could recoup once they made it to the other side.

He didn't know why they would come this far north though. It snowed for more than six months at a time, making it near on impossible to grow anything that would be worth eating. It might have made him think of home, if not for the freezing temperatures.

It was just as difficult to grow food where he was from, but it was because of the opposite temperature. Instead of it being too cold for most of the year, it was too hot instead.

All living plant life shrivelled and died within a matter of days as the heat soared during the hottest months of the year. There were only a few months where it was cool enough to grow anything. Which was one of the reasons why he didn't mind staying here.

Taredd made his way along the base of the mountain, looking for any indication that Humans had been in the area recently. Taredd had come across a few signs here and there, mainly footprints in the mud, but there was one spot that appeared to have been used as a campsite. Whether it was a Human campsite or not, was another question.

Other than that, it appeared none had been through this way for quite some time. Still, Taredd wasn't about to give up so easily, because he knew there was bound to be a few dotted around here somewhere.

When it started to get dark, as night fell, Taredd decided to make a camp. After all the alcohol he consumed last night with Dain and Arun, and with an early start tomorrow, he decided to catch up on some sleep. Unfortunately, he didn't have a soft mattress tonight, but he could improvise.

Taredd collected fallen leaves and handfuls of moss to make a bed, along with fallen twigs and branches to use for a fire. It wasn't exactly the soft and comfy bed he wanted, but it was better than sleeping on solid rock in the cave.

Taredd set up a trap not far away from where he was making camp, before building a fire. Once the fire was going and his bedding area pulled together, he sat back to admire the scenery. For such an unforgiving place, it had one of the most beautiful views he had ever seen.

After a couple of hours, Taredd went back to check on the trap. Luckily, he had left it long enough to catch something. He managed to snare a rabbit in the short time he had been away setting the fire and preparing a sleeping area.

Taredd untangled the animal before taking the trap

back down. Since he didn't need more than the one rabbit, there was absolutely no need to leave the trap up. He didn't want to get another animal caught in it unnecessarily. Grabbing the rabbit by the hind legs, he carried it back to camp.

It had never bothered Taredd to spend the night sleeping under the stars. As long as it stayed dry, he was happy. The last thing he wanted was to be woken during the night to rain, or worse, snow. Especially since he was a good few miles away from the nearest building where he could take shelter from the elements.

Yes, he could have gone to one of them instead of sleeping rough, but that would have wasted even more time. Taredd wasn't willing to travel to and fro each day just to have the luxury of sleeping indoors, that would just be a complete waste of his time.

Not only that, but if a Human was to come from the pass at any time of the day or night, he wanted to be here ready for them. He had set up his camp so that he would be the first to see them as they left the pass, but not so close that they would see him easily.

Since this was a bet after all, he was willing to take any advantage over Arun that he could. If that meant staying by the mountains, then so be it. After all, the sooner he won the bet, the sooner they could get back to hunting down Humans as a team again.

Taredd skinned and gutted the rabbit, then propped it over the fire to cook. It may not be the largest, or fanciest, of meals, but it was better than nothing at all. On the up side, Taredd was rather keen on the taste of rabbit, so it was a win win situation.

There was nothing better than cooking on an open fire while staring up at the twinkling stars up above. It was peaceful here, nothing but the sound of nature surrounded him. No talking, no bickering, nothing but peace and quiet, just what he needed at that moment in time.

Taredd had watched the sun set as the fire crackled next to him. Breathing in the cool air, he leaned back against a tree, relaxing while his food cooked. Listening to the birds singing in the trees as they settled in for the night, and mammals, as they scurried around on the ground. Some of them making their way into their burrows or dens for the night, while other nocturnal creatures were just waking up.

Closing his eyes, Taredd listened to all the sounds around him. He tried to identify where each sound was coming from, and what creature was making it. It wasn't something that Taredd would normally do, but since Dain and Arun weren't around to cause a racket, it was peaceful enough for him to do.

Taredd wondered how Arun was getting along in his search. He doubted Arun would find a Human before him, but on the off chance that he was wrong. Arun might be lucky and stumble across one, or even a group of Humans before him, but it was more likely that when Taredd finally met up with him again that he still wouldn't be anywhere close to finding one.

Not unless he recruited Dain to aid him in his search, but that was highly unlikely because Arun would see that as cheating. Arun had the same view of cheating as Taredd did, it was dishonourable. After all, there wasn't any point in making a bet if you weren't going to play fair. They may be a Demon and a Fae, but they still had their honour and they weren't about to throw it all away over a stupid bet.

The smell coming from the rabbit was making Taredd's mouth water. Not wanting to wait any longer, Taredd opened his eyes and sat up. Pulling a knife out of the sheaf strapped to his leg, he started cutting off bits of cooked meat.

"Mmm." He moaned as the flavour burst in his mouth.

Taredd savoured each bite before swallowing. It wasn't often he ate rabbit, so it was like a bit of luxury while camping rough.

Before long, his meal was finished. Taredd cleared away the remains, then rebuilt the fire before laying down on his makeshift bed. Stretching out next to the fire, he yawned and then rolled over onto his side so he could watch the flames dance as he drifted off to sleep.

CHAPTER TEN

Natalia

Natalia couldn't wait to finally be away from the freezing cold snow and ice of the mountains. Every time the sun had gone down, she'd had no choice but to find shelter in a cave for the night.

It was way too cold at night to travel, especially with the stupidly thin clothing she had on. But not just that, there was a higher probability that she was likely to take a wrong step in the dark, and knowing her luck it would be her last step.

Natalia hoped the others made it through okay. She would never forgive herself if anything happened to them. It was the thought of seeing them again soon that kept her going each day. As much as she had wanted to give up at times, she pushed through for Amberly and Donovan, if nothing else.

Each night, Natalia had pulled out every item of fabric she had in her satchel to try and keep herself warm enough to survive until morning. It was so cold at night that she half expected to not wake up every morning. Each time she laid down and closed her eyes she sent up a little prayer that she would make it another day, and each morning she was thankful that she woke up.

But the end was near, Natalia could see the end of the pass not far off in the distance, and it gave her the boost she needed to reach the end. She called on every last ounce of energy that she had left, and picked up the pace as much as she could.

Natalia didn't have a clue what she was going to do when she finally got there. She didn't know where the closest bunker to the mountain was located, and even if she did manage to find it, there was no guarantee Amberly, Donovan, and the rest of the group were going to be there.

As much as she wanted to find Amberly and Donovan straight away, she wasn't stupid or naive enough to think it was going to be a simple task. She wasn't lucky enough to find them as soon as she left the pass and she knew it.

Thinking rationally, the best course of action, was to find a bunker so she could recoup before heading out to find the others. Natalia had to admit, the thought of a nice long nap sounded perfect just about now. Preferably somewhere warm, where she could curl up under layers of blankets. Or at least somewhere she could build a fire to lay next to.

That was one of the things she should have been better prepared for before going along the pass. In hindsight, she should have collected some firewood for at night, but she'd been too preoccupied with needing to reach the others.

Next time though, firewood was going to be right at

the top of her list, along with warmer clothes and thicker blankets. Waterproof boots would definitely have come in handy as well, that's if she was able to scavenge some.

Natalia couldn't remember the last time she could feel her feet properly, which wasn't a good sign at all. But she was nearly at the other side now, so she could deal with her feet soon enough.

A cooked meal would go down a treat as well. Luckily enough, Natalia had found a small bag in one of the caves she had stayed in. She didn't know if it was left by Amberly and Donovan, but she was glad all the same.

Tucked away inside the bag had been a very small supply of bread and meat, there was even a couple of pieces of fruit as well. It was just enough to last her a day, maybe a little longer if she rationed it more than usual. Natalia didn't mind that there was only about a days' worth of food, because it was a days' worth more than what she had before she found it.

Natalia hoped the others hadn't set up camp too far away from the mountains. The closer they were to the mountains, the easier it would be to find them. Natalia hadn't come across any of their tracks along the pass, which was a good thing.

They all knew to hide any evidence of themselves before moving on, so even if she had stayed in some of the same caves as them, she wouldn't have known.. Plus, any footprints would have been covered over in the snow storm.

The closer she came to the end of the pass, the more

her feet began to drag along the floor. It felt as if she had weights tied to the bottom of her feet and they were getting heavier and heavier with each step she took. Natalia didn't care how difficult it got though, because one way or another she was going to make it. She was even prepared to crawl the rest of the way, if it came to it.

Not daring to stop just in case she couldn't get started again, she ploughed on as best she could. There was no way she was spending another night in this frozen wasteland., Finally, her hard work was paying off and she was rewarded when the snow turned to sludge before disappearing completely.

She had made it to the other side of the mountains, at last. Breathing a sigh of relief, she traipsed on a little further before she stopped for a rest. Making sure the earth was dry enough first, so she wouldn't get a wet ass, Natalia slid down next to a large tree to sit on the ground.

Leaning her head back against the tree, she closed her eyes for just a moment. At least, she thought it was for just a moment, but when she opened her eyes again the sun starting to set. Darkness was not her friend at the best of times, but even more so when she was alone and out in the open.

Natalia wasn't familiar with this area, so didn't have a clue where the closest bunker was located. Spending the night out in the open under the stars was not the wisest of ideas, but if she couldn't find anywhere soon, then she would have no other choice.

Pushing herself up from the floor, she stretched out

her aching muscles before picking up her satchel and heading off in search of a safe place to stay for the night. Even more so now than earlier it felt as if she had weights attracted to her feet, but it still wasn't enough to prevent her from looking for a bunker.

No matter how hard it became, she wouldn't stop even if her feet gave out on her. More than anything, Natalia needed to find a safe place to stay for the night. It didn't even need to be a bunker, but it had to be a hell of a lot safer than where she had been earlier.

Being out in the open like she had been was an extremely bad idea, especially when she didn't know the area. There was no telling how many monsters lived in the area, or where they were located. The last thing she want to do was to get caught because she was too close to where they lived.

Luckily enough though, Natalia didn't have to go very far before she found exactly what she was looking for, which was a really good thing because she didn't know how much longer she could physically stay on her feet.

The bad thing was, just as Natalia spotted the entrance to the bunker, she caught sight of movement out of the corner of her eye. As she spun around to see what it was, her eyes clashed with the black eyes of one of the monsters she was trying desperately to avoid.

Stuck like a deer in headlights, Natalia was frozen in place as they stared at each other. She didn't know who was more surprised, her or the monster. By the look on his face, he appeared just as shocked to see her as she was him.

There was no doubt in her mind that it was a male that stood before her. The size and shape of him gave it away that he was in fact a he without having to see his face close up.

Taller than any Human she's ever seen by a long shot, he had dark red skin and black hair. His thick head of hair couldn't hide the horns that protruded from the top of its head. Natalia was glad it was still just before nightfall, because if it had been completely dark, then there would have been no way in hell she could have seen it.

Dressed all in black, he would have easily blended into the night. Natalia might even have mistaken him for a shadow, or even thought that her mind was playing tricks on her. Which, after the last couple of days with barely any food or sleep, it was a high possibility that it could have just been her imagination.

Natalia was jolted into action as he took a step towards her. Spinning on her heels, she darted to the entrance of the bunker. Hoping with everything in her that she made it in time.

CHAPTER ELEVEN

Taredd

Taredd knew staying in the area would pay off eventually, and he hadn't been wrong. It did take slightly longer than he had originally thought it would, but it still paid off in the end.

Not even a week after restarting the bet with Arun, he had finally found a Human, and it was a female. It was only the one, but generally where there was one, there was more. Taredd wasn't interested in finding more at the moment. If he did, then bonus, but if not, it wasn't a big deal. Either way, he had won the bet.

Now all he needed to do was catch the slippery little fucker. For a female, she was extremely fast and agile on her feet, disappearing from view before he had a chance to get anywhere close to her.

Humans weren't normally so fast. He'd never come across a Human that had managed to disappear on him, especially not a female. So, Taredd had a sneaking suspicion that there must be a hideout around here somewhere. If he could just locate it, then he was positive he would find her.

With that thought in mind, Taredd decided to search

the area with a fine-tooth comb while there was still a little bit of daylight left. Walking over to where he had spotted her, Taredd searched the immediate area. He was just about to widen the search area when the setting sun glinted of something on the ground, hidden beneath a bush.

Taredd walked over and moved the bush aside. He couldn't believe his eyes. In all the years he had been hunting down the Humans, it never occurred to him that they might be living underground. But the proof was staring him straight in the face.

A small circular disk was sticking out of the ground. It was just about wide enough for him to fit through, and he was much larger than most Humans, so it would be a perfect size for them.

Taredd didn't know for sure if she was down there, but it was the only explanation he could think of as to how she managed to disappear so quickly.

On closer inspection, Taredd noticed that it had a curved handle sticking out on one side. If this was definitely how the Humans had been hiding from them, then it was going to be a complete game changer. Especially if there was more than two or three in there.

That's how they were usually caught, in twos or threes at a time. Trying to find more than that in one go was like trying to find a needle in a haystack. But if they were living underground in larger groups... well then, that would mean they could be rounded up much easier. It would also mean that the end of their existence could be a lot sooner than he thought.

All they would have to do is look for these little disks to find where they were taking shelter. These things were bound to be far easier to find than the Humans, especially since these things didn't move around like the humans did. At least, not that he could see.

Leaning down, Taredd was about to pull the handle up when he stopped himself. Changing his mind at the last minute, he decided to watch for any other Humans. Instead of going in there straight away... and winning the bet... he wanted to see if anyone else came or went.

So, moving further away, Taredd positioned himself so that he could easily see the area with the disk but without anyone being able to see him. Then, he waited.

CHAPTER TWELVE

Natalia

Natalia's heart was racing so fast she thought it might explode from her chest. She knew without a shadow of a doubt that he was still out there. She didn't have a clue how she knew it, but that didn't change the fact that she did.

The question was, did he know she was in here? And if so, then why wasn't he coming in after her? It didn't make any sense. Unless he was waiting for something, but then if that was the case, then what was he waiting for?

If he was waiting for her to go out to him, then he would be waiting a long time. The same goes for if he was waiting for another one of her kind to either leave or arrive. Natalia just hoped that he wasn't out there waiting for more of his kind to arrive.

It would be really bad news for her if that was the case. All she could do, was hope and pray that he hadn't found her hiding place, had given up the search, and was now on his way back to wherever it was he came from.

When her heart finally stopped racing, Natalia

explored the new bunker. It wasn't much different from all the other ones she has stayed in over the years. It consisted of one main living area, a sleeping area, and a small washroom.

Luckily enough for her, whoever it had been that stayed here prior to her arrival had left plenty of food and water. It was more than enough to last her a good couple of days at least, even longer if she rationed it well.

After that she would have no choice but to leave the bunker, or starve to death... which definitely wasn't an option she was willing to even consider. Especially not when Amberly and Donovan counted on her so much.

Natalia didn't know what she was going to do about Amberly and Donovan. She knew it wasn't them that had been the last people to stay here, Amberly would have left some form of clue if they had been. So, where were they? Was there another bunker close by? Or were they still along the pass?

Natalia knew they wouldn't have moved too far away from the pass if they didn't need to, they would want to be as close as possible so she could find them easily enough, and she hoped to hell that they weren't still on the pass.

Each day they spent traveling along the mountain pass increased their chances of not making it through alive. Now Natalia wished she had taken the time to checked each of the caves on her way past them, just in case they were still taking shelter in one.

If they had made it and were just staying in a different bunker, then she hoped they didn't decide to go looking for her. If the monster was still out there, like she had a feeling he was, then they could get caught by him and that was the last thing she wanted to happen.

What if they were already caught by him though? It was possible that Amberly and Donovan had been staying here but had been caught. She hoped that wasn't the case, but until she found them, she wouldn't know.

If they had been, then was that why he was still here? Was he waiting to see if any more Humans were in the area and she just happened to appear at the perfect moment?

She didn't know, but, it was just her kind of dumb luck that it would be something along those lines. Natalia hoped that the others were as far away from here as possible. The last thing she wanted was for them to be captured and killed. Natalia would never forgive herself if anything happened to any of them, but especially Amberly and Donovan.

Agitated, Natalia wanted to head straight back out to look for them, but she knew it would be the biggest mistake of her life if she did. If the monster was still out there looking for her and hadn't found where she was hiding, then her leaving the bunker so soon after being seen would definitely give away her location, if he was still looking for her.

Not only that, but if he hadn't seen where she went, then it would also show the monsters how they had managed to stay hidden after all this time. She couldn't be the one to give away the secret to the survival of the Human race. It would ultimately mean that she had caused the end of their species, and that was not going to be what she was remember for. Not that there would be anyone left to remember her, but still, it wasn't going to happen. At least, not if she could help it.

No, as much as she hated it, she was better off staying where she was for as long as she could. She had enough food to hopefully out last him, and once he was gone then she could safely go outside and find the others. She just hoped they didn't go in search of her and get themselves caught in the meantime.

Amberly and Donovan weren't stupid though, but she couldn't stop worrying about them. She needed to stop thinking that they were going to get caught without her there to keep them safe. She needed to trust that they would do what needed to be done. Even if it meant she would never see them again.

She knew they were both more than capable of not only looking out for themselves and each other, but also everyone else in the group. Natalia wouldn't have gotten everyone in the group as far as she had if it hadn't been for Amberly and Donovan standing by her side every step of the way. They didn't know it because she's never told them, but they were the reason she carried on each day, and the reason she climbed out of bed each day.

If it hadn't been for them supporting her every step of the way, then she would have broken down and given up years ago. But they wouldn't let her, they forced her to face each new day as it came and she would eternally love them for it because it made her a better person. A person her mother would have been proud of.

They made sure that she not only took care of everyone else, but that she took care of herself as well. They made sure she didn't miss a single meal and that she had plenty of sleep each night, even going so far as to taking over her night shifts when it had been a long few days with little sleep.

Natalia grabbed a bowl from the kitchen area and filled it half way with hot water. She needed to clean and bandage the wounds on her feet before they got infected. She knew with all the walking she had done over the last couple of days that her feet were going to be covered in cuts and blisters. Plus, she still needed to warm them up because at the moment they were so cold she could barely feel or move them.

Her socks and boots were both soaked through, which was preventing her feet from warming up on their own. She knew if she didn't deal with them quickly, then she wasn't going to be able to walk on them at all very soon.

Carefully carrying the bowl of water over to the table, she set in down on the floor in front of a chair. She took her coat off and hung it on the back of the chair before taking a seat.

Slowly, one by one Natalia took off her boots, wincing at the pain it caused. She placed them on the floor under the table before gently sliding off her socks. Natalia noticed cuts and blisters all over her feet from where the boots had rubbed so badly against them as she had walked.

They were also starting to turn a bluish shade as well, which wasn't a good sign. Natalia hoped the hot water helped fix the problem, if not she didn't know what she was going to do.

Natalia gingerly placed her feet in the water to help warm them up and get the blood flowing, as well as clean some of the cuts. Thankfully, as her feet began to warm up, she started to get some feeling back in them.

Opening one of the bottles of water she had found, Natalia gulped it down as she leaned back, relaxing into the chair. It wasn't exactly the life of luxury, but it sure beat the hell out of sleeping rough in a freezing cold cave for another night.

Placing the bottle on the table , she closed her eyes and rolled her head to stretch the tense muscles in her neck and then did the same for her shoulders. The feeling in her feet was returning with a vengeance. Pain radiated from her toes and the balls of her feet, through her arches to her heels.

Bending down she gently scrubbed them clean, and then lifted them out of the water to dry them off. Before she pulled on a clean and dry pair of socks, she rubbed antiseptic cream into all the cuts and wrapped them in bandages.

Natalia bit her lip as the cream caused the open wounds to sting. She would rather put up with this slight pain than deal with an infection later on if she did nothing to prevent it now.

Pushing the bowl to one side when she was finished, Natalia then stood and made her way to the bedroom.

After the last few days of getting little to no sleep at all, she was more than ready to get a good night's sleep.

Settling for the first bed she came to. Natalia pulled out her blanket and pillow from her satchel, she laid them out on the bed before grabbing the pile of blankets that were folded neatly on the top bunk and doing the same with them.

Natalia didn't go anywhere without her blanket. It didn't matter that it was old and tatty because her mother had made it for her when she was little, so no matter what it looked like, she would always keep it.

She lifted the blankets to climb underneath them, then curled up on her side. Not long after her head hit the pillow, she was fast asleep.

CHAPTER THIRTEEN

Taredd

Taredd waited in his hiding spot until late the following night, but not once did he see any other Humans coming or going. Even the female from the night before hadn't shown herself again. In fact, other than the local wildlife, he hadn't seen another living being in the area the entire time he had been sat there.

When the sun had set, and night had shrouded the area in darkness, he decided it was time to make his move. Taredd made sure to keep the entrance in his sights at all times as he searched the ground for anything he might have missed the night before. Once he was completely satisfied there wasn't anything else to find, he walked back over to the entrance.

As he inspected the area more closely, Taredd didn't see any peepholes of any kind. How the Humans expected to know if it was safe to leave or not without something to look out of was beyond him. That would be one of the first things he did if he was in their shoes.

He checked around the circular disk for a latch of some kind, that might be keeping it locked. When he didn't find any, he tested the handle. It was easier than he had expected to lifted up the hatch, but he should have known it wouldn't be too difficult. It was a Human hideout and they were a lot weaker than the rest of the species.

Apart from the light shining down and a slight squeaking of the hinges as he opened it, there was no other indication that anyone else was here. Taredd listened intently for any sounds that were coming from down below before he opened the hatch wide enough for him to fit through.

When he didn't hear anything, he laid the hatch on the ground and inspected the tunnel that lead down. There was a metal ladder sticking out on one side of the entrance, and Taredd could see a tunnel leading away.

There was no light coming from anywhere inside the tunnel that he could see, but that meant nothing. There could still be a bunch of Humans hiding out inside, or at least the female he had spotted the other day. If she wasn't down here, then he didn't have a clue where the fuck she had disappeared to, but he was certainly going to find out where she was hiding.

Knowing Taredd's luck, she was probably going to be the Human Arun would find if she wasn't down there. If that did turn out to be the case, then there was no way in hell he was going to tell either Arun or Dain that he spotted her first.

He would never hear the end of it from either of them that a Human female had escaped from him. Not only losing the bet to Arun, but to also let a Human...

especially a female one... slip through his fingers would be the ultimate humiliation.

With that thought in mind, Taredd quietly lowered himself into the tunnel and descended the ladder.

***

He was coming in.

Natalia could hear the hatch to the bunker as it was opened and froze at the sound, unsure whether to run or hide. Not that there was anywhere she could run to. For that matter, there wasn't exactly many places she could hide in here either. The only thing she could do was to find a cupboard or something that was big enough for her to fit inside.

That was easier said than done when there was only a handful of cupboards, none of which were big enough for her to fit inside, a child maybe, but definitely not an adult.

Natalia just hoped that he turned out to be a stupid monster that didn't look in every nook and cranny. If he did, then there was no doubt she would be found, and easily since the only place she could hide was under one of the beds.

After all, this entire bunker was supposed to be their hiding place. They didn't expect the monsters to find them down here, but in hindsight they probably should have prepared for it anyway. They should have known that it was only a matter of time before their hiding places were exposed. They were lucky to have lasted this long without it being found.

Natalia never thought in her wildest dreams that she would be the one responsible for giving away their location. If anything, Natalia thought it would have been Bella that ultimately gave it away. But no, it appeared it was going to be her fault, and now she had to deal with the consequences of her actions.

With her hiding choices limited to either behind the sofa or under the bed, Natalia didn't hold out much hope of not being found. The bunker only had three rooms, one of which was a bedroom with a couple of built-in bunk beds. The largest was the living space which had a table and chairs, and a small kitchen area with a couple of small cupboards.

The only other room in the place was the washroom, a tiny little room with a toilet and sink. It was barely big enough to stand up and turn around in that room. So, the only place big enough for her to fit, and didn't involve her moving furniture around, was under one of the beds.

So, she was well and truly up shit creek without a paddle. There was no way in hell he was going to come down here and not find her. She might as well save them both some time and just hand herself over to him now, but she wasn't going to make it that easy for him.

If he thought for one second that she was going to go down without a fight, then he was sorely mistaken. Natalia was going to go out fighting if it came to it, she didn't stand a hope in hell of winning, but she certainly wasn't going to go down quietly.

It would be fantastic if she could take out one of the

monsters at the same time, but that was highly unlikely. Even if she did know how to fight, she still wouldn't be able to take out one of them, even the weakest of their kind were too strong for her to take on.

If entire armies of Humans with a multitude of weapons that were readily available couldn't defeat them, then what could a single woman on her own with nothing but a knife do to them? Absolutely fuck all, that was the answer. Maybe piss them off a bit, but there was no way she could cause them any harm.

Natalia raced into the bedroom when she heard him begin to descend the ladder. Laying down next to the bed furthest away from the door, she shuffled as quickly and quietly as she could across the floor until she was pressed up as tightly against the wall.

Staying as still and silent as possible, she listened to his footsteps as he moved around in the other room.

Shit!

Natalia remembered that she had left the bowl of water next to the chair. That was bound to be a dead giveaway someone had been staying here, and recently as well. She could have kicked herself if it wouldn't have given away her position.

Trust her to leave shit lying around, and trust her to be the one that finally showed the monsters how and where they had been hiding from them for all these years. If Natalia ever got herself out of this position, she swore to be a better, kinder, and more considerate person.

Natalia sucked in a breath when the door opened

and he walked in.

CHAPTER FOURTEEN

Taredd

Taredd didn't waste any time in climbing to the bottom of the ladder. He didn't know what to expect when he reached the bottom, but it certainly wasn't a small room the shape of a tin can.

How anybody in their right mind managed to stay down here without going stir crazy was beyond him. No air flowed through, and there was very little natural light that reached this far down. Luckily enough he found a light switch just inside the room, but the tunnel between the entrance at the top of the ladder and this room there was nothing except what shone through the open grate.

There was hardly any furniture in this room, which was a good thing since it wasn't the largest of spaces. What passed as their kitchen area, was just three cupboards and a work top, that was it. The only other items in the room, was a small table with a couple of chairs dotted round it and a ratty looking sofa and arm chair.

What caught Taredd's attention most though, was the bowl of water on the floor just under the table next to one of the chairs. He wondered why someone would feel the need to put a bowl of water there, they must have a good reason for it, but he couldn't think of a single thing.

There was another door at the opposite end of the room from the stairs. Intrigued to know what was on the other side of the door, Taredd didn't hesitate to open it and find out.

This room wasn't much better than the other. It was a similar size and shape, but the only things in here were beds... and not very large ones at that. Taredd would have a hard time fitting on one of these beds, they looked more suited to children than adults. He had to admit though, that Humans were shorter than any of the other species.

Taredd didn't know how many Humans stayed down here at any given time, but there were only eight beds, stacked in twos on either side of the room. If there were any more than that, did that mean they slept on the floor?

To be honest, Taredd wouldn't want to stay down here with just two people, let alone eight or more. It was probably because he was a good foot and a half taller than most of the Humans he has come across, but it was way too small in here for his liking. Even if he was shorter, he wouldn't want to stay down here for any longer than necessary.

It was cold and dirty down here, plus it made him feel as if he was in a can of food. Why on earth anyone would want to live in these conditions was beyond him.

Taredd wondered if the Human female was in fact down here. She wasn't in either of the rooms as far as he could see, and there weren't many other places she could hide. There was only one other door in the place that he hadn't look inside of yet, but he wasn't holding his breath that she was in there either.

As soon as he opened the door, he knew for sure that he had assumed right. The size of a small cupboard, the only things in this room were a toilet and sink. Definitely not a hiding space. So, unless there was a secret passage that he hasn't found, then there was no place down here to hide. Which meant he has spent nearly two days hanging around for nothing when he could have been looking elsewhere.

No, she had to be here somewhere, there was nowhere else she could have gone. He knew that for sure because he had searched the area and the only footprints, he had found of hers were right next to the entrance to this place. He hadn't found any other tracks than the ones that lead him to here, so she must be around here somewhere. There had to be something he was missing, but what was it?

Taredd walked back into the other room and followed his footsteps back to the ladder so he could check that there wasn't anything he had missed, but there was nothing. No secret hatch, latch, or anything.

Going back into the bedroom, he moved further into the room this time and was about to check under the beds. As he neared the far end of the room, he heard the slightest sound of movement coming from under one of the beds. If he hadn't been listening intently, he could have easily missed it, but luckily enough he had been.

"Hmm, looks like there's nobody home," he said aloud. "I suppose I best get going, there's no point in wasting any more time here."

Taredd had no intention of leaving the underground hovel, but he wanted the person under the bed to think he was. So, turning on his heels he quickly vacated the room, remembering to shut the door again as he left.

As he made his way over to the ladder, he didn't try to be quiet because he wanted her to hear him and think he was leaving. When he reached the ladder, he noisily climbed up the steps. Half way up he changed direction, but he made it appear as if he was still leaving.

By the time he reached the bottom again he was barely making any sound at all. As far as the female was concerned, she would think he was no longer down here with her.

Sneaking back over to the bedroom door, he stood to one side and waited patiently for the female to crawl out from under the bed and exit the room.

It didn't take as long as he expected before he could hear movement coming from the room. It was only a matter of time before she was going to step out of there to see if the coast was clear. He was ready to pounce when she did.

The door slowly crept open, and as he had assumed, the female from the day before stepped out. Without hesitating, Taredd pounced. Grabbing her by the shirt, he swiftly pulled her off her feet and threw her to the ground. Using his body to pin her in place so she couldn't escape, not that she would get very far with him chasing after her, but still, he wasn't willing to risk her disappearing on him again.

Unlike last time though, she only had one place she could go and he was more than capable of stopping her before she even came close to reaching the ladder.

"I have you now, little Human," he told her.

"Get off me, you monster!" She shouted as she squirmed underneath him.

"Fight as much as you like, you're not getting away from me again," he told her.

"Of course not with you laying on top of me, you great fucking lump," she snapped. "Do you weigh a ton, or what?"

Taredd laughed. He couldn't help it, because she had a lot of fire for a Human.

"I'm not that heavy," he said. "You would know about it if I was."

Most of the ogres weighed more than a tonne, and Taredd had seen first-hand what a Human looked like after one had sat on them. It wasn't a pretty sight.

"Well, you're heavy enough to limit my breathing," she said, trying in vein to push him off her.

"If I was limiting your breathing, then you wouldn't be talking now, would you?" he said.

"Smart arse," she mumbled.

"Why, thank you," he said smugly.

"That wasn't a compliment," she said adamantly. "Just get off me, already."

"Nope," he said, shaking his head. "I can't do that

because you'll try to run away."

"Well, of course," she said. "I'm not just going to stand still and let you kill me, am I? Why would I make it easier on you?"

"I'm not going to kill you." That got her attention, and she instantly stopped struggling.

"Why not?" she asked, perplexed.

"Because then I'd have to carry you," he said honestly.

Yeah, on hindsight he probably shouldn't have told her that because as soon as the last word left his mouth, she started struggling to get away from him again.

"Just stop already," he told her. "You're not going to get me off you like that."

"Well, I'm certainly not going to go anywhere with you willingly," she said. "If that's what you think, then you're sorely mistaken."

"That's exactly what I think, and that's exactly what's going to happen," he told her. "Whether you like it or not."

Stopping again, she asked: "Why?"

"Why what?" he asked.

"Why do you need me to go with you?" she asked. "Why aren't you going to kill me straight away like your kind normally does?"

"Because..."

"Because what?" she prompted when he didn't continue.

Taredd wasn't sure if to tell her the truth, or to lie to her. Either way, he didn't think she was going to like the answer, so he decided on the truth.

"Because I have a bet going with my friends," he told her blatantly.

"What? Is it on who's a better killer?" she asked sarcastically.

"No, it's nothing like that," he said.

"Then like what?" she asked.

"Who can catch a Human the quickest." Saying it out loud like that made it sound pretty stupid, but what else could he say? It was something to do to pass the time, and at the end of the day it wasn't even his idea.

"Congratulations to you if you're the winner. I would clap but... my hands are kinda stuck at the moment," she said sarcastically.

"Oh, it will be me," he said confidently.

"Big headed or what."

Taredd couldn't see her face from this position, but he could just imagine that she was rolling her eyes when she said that.

"I'm not big headed. I'm honest," he said.

"Yeah, right," she said, and again he could picture her rolling her eyes.

"I'm telling the truth," he told her. "I am a better hunter than he is. So, it's not being big headed, it's stating a fact."

"If it's a fact, then why do you have a bet going with him in the first place?" she asked.

"For entertainment, why else?"

She was silent for a moment before finally saying: "So, because you and your buddy are bored, you thought it would be a good idea to hunt down my kind?"

"Something like that, yes," he admitted.

"Great, just great."

"What else would you have us do?" he asked.

"Well, not kill my kind would be a great start."

"I already told you, I'm not going to kill you."

"Yet, anyway," she countered.

After another moments silence, he asked: "Are you going to try running away as soon as I get up?"

"Yes," she said without hesitation.

"Why?" he asked. "You know I'll just catch you again."

"Because..."

"Because what?" he asked when she didn't finish this time.

"Why do you think?" she asked him, but before he could answer her, she added "Because I don't want to die."

"What if I promised that you wouldn't die?"

Taredd didn't know why he said that, it wasn't something he has ever said to a Human before. But then, he's never spoken to a Human this much before either. So, it appeared it was going to be a day of firsts all around for him.

"You would promise that?" she asked.

"Yes," he said.

"But... why?" she asked, confused.

"Because I can." Taredd didn't know why, so he couldn't give her any other answer.

She thought about it for a moment before she replied: "Okay, I won't run."

"Do you promise?"

Huffing out a breath, she said: "Yes, I promise I won't run away from the monster, just like a good little girl."

"I'm not a monster," he told her. "I'm a Demon."

"And that's supposed to make it better?" she asked.

"Yes."

"Well, it doesn't," she said. "So, are you going to get off me then, or what?"

"Of course," he said but he still didn't budge right away.

He wasn't completely convinced that she wasn't going to try to escape, even with her promising not to he still didn't totally believe her.

"Well? Come on then, get the fuck off me," she said, trying to roll him off her. "I wasn't joking when I said you were fucking heavy."

"Fine, but don't run," he told her again.

"I already said I wouldn't, didn't I?"

Taredd didn't believe her for one moment, but he still climbed off her. Once on his feet, Taredd held out his hand for her to take, but she swatted it away.

"About bloody time," she said, climbing to her feet and brushing herself off.

Taredd couldn't help but smile. For such a small thing, she had a lot of fire in her, and that impressed the hell out of him.

CHAPTER FIFTEEN

Natalia

Natalia couldn't believe it. How the hell did she manage to get herself caught by possibly the only Demon in the world who has ever promised not to kill a Human?

She was positive that he had planned to kill her in the beginning, but then changed his mind. But why? Was it just because he couldn't be bothered carrying her dead body to prove to his friends that he had in fact caught one of her kind?

Natalia didn't know the answer to any of the questions floating around in her mind, but then again, she didn't really care what the reason was either. At the end of the day, if he wasn't going to kill her, then she wasn't going to complain about it.

The question now was, were his friends going to do the killing for him? Was that the real reason he wasn't going to kill her? If that's what he planned, then he could think again. As far as she was concerned, he promised she wouldn't die, and that meant by his friends' hands as well.

"You don't have to look so smug about it," she told

him.

"I don't look smug," he said.

"Of course, you do. Otherwise your face wouldn't be doing that," she said, pointing her finger at his lips... his kissable lips.

Whoa, where did that come from? Natalia thought as she mentally slapped herself.

Nothing about him was kissable, he was a monster through and through, and she had to remember that.

"Are you saying that I'm not allowed to smile?" he asked, still grinning at her.

"That's exactly what I'm saying, especially if that's what you call a smile," she told him.

If for no other reason than to keep her own sanity, because god that smile affected her more than she cared to admit. It was a mix of saint and sinner, tempting her to lean in for a taste.

Natalia gave herself a mental slap. How she could find a Demon attractive she didn't know, but there was something about this one that got her all hot and bothered, and it had nothing to do with him pinning her to the floor a moment ago.

Well, I could blame it on lack of sleep, she thought. *Maybe I banged my head somewhere along the line and just didn't realize.*

Now she was grasping at straws and she knew it, but she wasn't prepared to accept that she found a Demon attractive, even if it was just to herself.

"Of course it's a smile, what else would it be?" he laughed.

"Looks more like a smirk to me," she lied, because

there was no way in hell, she was going to admit the truth.

"Well, you obviously haven't seen many smiles in your life before, then."

"There's not really much to smile about when you're constantly on the run for your life, now is there?" she asked.

"Yeah, I suppose you haven't had much to smile about, have you," he said, finally dropping the smile from his face.

Natalia had a really weird feeling that she had just upset him, but the weirdest thing about it was she wanted to take it back so he would smile at her again. But that was just plain stupid.

Why on earth should she care if she hurt his feelings or not? After all, his kind - and even he - openly hunted and killed her kind and they didn't give a shit if they hurt anyone's feeling, so why should she?

"So, where are you taking me?" she asked, trying to change the subject.

She didn't want to look too deeply into why hurting his feelings affected her so much, so it was safer just to think about something else instead.

"I don't know yet," he told her.

"You don't know where your friends are?" she asked.

"No."

"So, what? We're just going to wonder around until we find them?" she asked. When he nodded his head, she added: "No wonder you didn't want to carry me the whole time."

"It shouldn't take too long to find them," he said.

"Do you even know where to start looking?" she asked with a raised brow.

"I have a rough idea of which direction they went in," he said.

"At least that's something, I suppose," she said.

Not only that, but the further they had to travel to reach his friends, the more opportunities Natalia would have to escape him. Because even though she promised not to, that was the first thing she was going to do the first chance she got.

"Let's go then," he said.

"It's dark outside."

"And?"

Shaking her head, she said: "I don't know about you, but I can't see very well in the dark, so I'm not going anywhere until morning."

"I don't think you understand," he told her. "I'm not giving you a choice in the matter. We are leaving now, and we will travel for as long as I say."

"Bossy much?" she asked.

"No, I just don't want to waste any more time. Especially not cooped up in a tin can," he said, looking around the room. "If you're worried about not being able to see in the dark, then don't because I can see clearly enough for the both of us. Now let's go."

"Fine!" She snapped. "Can I at least get my stuff together first?"

The Demon looked around the bare room, then looked at her as if she had gone mad.

"What stuff?" he asked. "The place is empty."

"Well, I couldn't leave everything lying around for you to find, could I?" she asked. "I was hiding from you after all."

Seriously, how dumb could this Demon be?

"That's true," he agreed.

"How did you know I was here?" she asked, intrigued to know the answer.

"I heard you," he said blatantly.

"Seriously? I didn't make any noise, I didn't even move," she told him.

"Yes, seriously. I know you didn't move," he said. "I heard you exhale."

What the fuck?

Natalia filed that bit of information away for future reference. From now on, she knew not to breath too loudly, otherwise she was going to get caught again. That's if she managed to get away from him in the first place.

"Fine," he relented. "Get your stuff together, but be quick about it."

"Thanks," she said, rolling her eyes as she walked back into the bedroom. When she realized he was following her, she asked: "Where are you going?"

"With you, of course."

"Why? It's not like there's anywhere for me to go in here," Natalia said.

"How would I know?" he said, looking around the room. "There could be a secret passageway somewhere in here."

"Well, for starters, I wouldn't have been hiding under the bed if there was," she told him.

"You might have thought I wouldn't find you there," he said.

She wasn't about to tell him that she had hoped he wouldn't have looked under the bed. So instead, she said: "Yeah right, because who wouldn't think to look under the bed?"

From the look on his face, it was clear he had planned to look under the bed, but she gave away her location before he had the chance to.

"I'm not that stupid, you know," she told him. "It's not as if I'm spoilt for choice when it comes to hiding places."

Natalia grabbed her coat and satchel from under the bed where she had been hiding. She put her coat on and then draped the strap of the satchel over her shoulder before turning to face the Demon again.

"Is that it?" he asked, looking at her meager belongings.

"Well, yeah," she said. "This kind of life doesn't make it easy for carrying around a load of shit, you know. Everything I own needs to be easy to move at a moment's notice, and it has to be easy enough to run with if need be."

"I understand."

"I don't think you do," she said, shaking her head. "How could you when you've never been hunted like I have?"

"Just because I'm a Demon, doesn't mean I've never been hunted before."

"Yeah, right," she said, rolling her eyes.

"Believe what you want," he said. "But it's the

truth."

"If it's the truth, then why do you hunt down and murder my kind?" When he didn't reply, she added: "Yeah, I didn't think so."

"Come on," he said after a moment. "We need to get going now."

"I still don't understand why we can't wait until morning," she said, but then it finally twigged on her. "You want to leave now so that your friend has less chance of winning the bet, don't you?"

"I've already won the bet," he said adamantly.

"How do you know?" she asked. "He could have captured one of us and you wouldn't even know about it because you're here with me."

"There's no way Arun has caught a Human already," he said, shaking his head.

"Why not? You have." It was the first time he's mentioned a name, but it still wasn't his.

"Because he's not that good of a hunter, that's why."

"But you are?" she asked sceptically.

"Yes," he stated.

"Because you're a Demon?" she asked.

"Partly, but mostly because I am just a better hunter than him."

"Okay then, whatever you say, Demon," she said, rolling her eyes.

"My name isn't Demon," he told her.

"And?"

"I would rather you call me by my name than refer to me as Demon all the time."

"Would you like me to just guess your name?" she

asked sarcastically. "Because you certainly haven't told me what it is."

"I could say the same to you," he said pointedly.

"So?" she said, glaring at him.

At the end of the day, why would she be willing to tell him her name when he'd intended on killing her? She wouldn't. It didn't matter that he'd changed his mind and was now kidnapping her instead. The jury was still out on whether that was a good thing or not.

"Fine, I'll go first. My name is Taredd, and your name is?" He raised an eyebrow at her expectantly.

"Natalia," she said reluctantly.

"It's nice to meet you, Natalia," he said, then smiled at her.

The way her name rolled of his tongue sent shivers down her spine. Never before had she had such an effect just from someone saying her name, and she didn't like it one bit. Well, she did, but she certainly wasn't going to admit it aloud - ever.

"I would say it's nice to meet you, but, you know," she said, shrugging her shoulder. "That would be lying and my mom always taught me not to lie."

"Well, the pleasure is all mine then," he said, flashing that wicked smile at her again.

"Great, you can keep all the pleasure," she told him, trying to ignore the butterflies in her stomach at the same time.

There was no way in hell she was going to show how he affected her, and she certainly wasn't going to tell him that this was the most entertainment she's had in a long time. Nope, those things she was going to keep to herself.

Natalia had to admit, it was kind of nice not having anyone come running to her with problems to resolve, or constantly worrying about everyone else. And it only took getting caught by a Demon for that to finally happen.

CHAPTER SIXTEEN

Taredd

Taredd didn't have a clue why he promised Natalia that she wasn't going to die, ultimately all Humans did, it was just a fact of life. As much as he didn't understand his reasons, he couldn't deny the fact that she was entertaining. He didn't know if all Humans were this entertaining, because he'd never spoken to one before. Let alone bantered with one like he was with her.

To be honest, it was a welcome relief to know that she wasn't some blubbering idiot that was going to cry their eyes out the whole time. He quite enjoyed her sass, and for a Human, she was extremely attractive. So, he was finding it really easy to keep his promise to her.

Taredd didn't think it would be the same way with any of the other Humans, but then again, he could be wrong. Especially since he had been so completely wrong about this one.

For starters, he hadn't thought she would have put up such a fight when he had her pinned face down on the floor. But she wasn't giving up without a fight, even though she must have known she didn't stand a chance of overpowering him. Yet, she still tried to break free. He couldn't' help but admire her for that.

Not many Humans would have done the same thing, and definitely not any of the females that he'd come across. Most of them seemed to accept their fate willingly, but not Natalia. No, if given the chance, he could imagine her fighting tooth and nail to stay alive, and he couldn't blame her. Taredd wouldn't go quietly either.

"So, how far do you think we have to go?" she asked as she headed towards the ladder.

"I'm not sure."

"You're not even going to guess?" she asked.

He could, but there was no point. Arun and Dain could be absolutely anywhere by now, and since he didn't think she would like that answer, he said: "No."

"Why not?" she persisted.

"Because it doesn't matter where they are," he told her. "It'll take as long as it takes."

Stopping at the bottom of the ladder, she turned to him and asked: "How long has it been since you saw them last?"

"A couple of days."

"Is that it?" she asked.

"Yes, that's it," he said. Then, stopping her as she reached for the ladder, he told her: "I'll go first."

"Why? Don't you trust me?" she asked.

"No, I don't," he told her honestly.

"But I already told you I wouldn't run off."

Yeah, right, he thought before he said aloud:"That

doesn't mean you won't try though."

"So, you expect me to trust your word that you won't kill me, yet you're not willing to trust that I won't run off? That seems a bit unfair, don't you think?" she said.

"It doesn't matter if it's fair or not," he said. "That's the way it is."

"Fine!" she snapped, stepping out of the way. Holding her hand out towards the ladder, she added: "By all means, go first."

"Thank you," Taredd said as he took the lead.

"So, what are you going to do with me when you need to sleep?" she asked as she followed him. "Are you going to tie me to a tree or something?"

Taredd couldn't deny the thought had crossed his mind. "No, I don't need much sleep, so that will not be a problem."

"What about when I sleep?" she asked.

"I'm sure I can keep an eye on you while you're asleep," he said confidently.

"So, you're not going to sleep at the same time as me then?"

"I already told you, I don't need a lot of sleep," he said, holding his hand out to help her when she reached the top, but just like before, she batted it away. "We will more than likely find my friends before I need to sleep next."

"Seriously?" she asked, looking surprised by his answer as she closed the lid on the underground hovel.

"Yes, seriously."

Once she was ready, they started walking in the

direction he had last seen Arun and Dain.

"But you said you don't know where your friends are, so it could take days to find them for all you know."

"That's very true," he agreed. "But that doesn't change my answer. I can go long periods of time without any sleep."

"Wow! I need sleep every night," she said. "At least six hours' worth, or I'm like a zombie all day."

"What's a zombie?" he asked, confused.

"It's like a dead person walking around."

"Really? Like a Vampire?" he asked, raising both eyebrows.

"Yeah, really," she told him. "But nothing like a Vampire. Zombies come back to life and eat people."

"That I'd like to see," Taredd said. "I've never seen a dead person get up once they're dead."

"I bet you've seen a lot of dead people," she said.

"Yes, I have," he said.

"I bet you also killed most of them, didn't you?" she said.

"I've killed my fair share, yes, I don't deny that," he told her honestly, but added defensively: "But did I kill them all? No, I didn't."

"Okay, then," she dragged out the words before she added: "No need to get your knickers in a twist."

"I don't wear knickers," he said, disgusted at the idea of wearing female underwear.

"For fuck sake, it's only a saying." She laughed.

"Well, how was I supposed to know? It's just like your zombie comment," he told her. "Where the hell did that come from anyway?"

"Oh, I read it in a book once," she said.

"Really? You can read?"

Natalia punched him in the arm. Taredd didn't know if she intended on hurting him, but it didn't come anywhere close.

"What was that for?" he asked.

"Yes, I can read," she told him angrily.

"I'm sorry if I offended you, but I didn't think any of your kind could still read after all these years," he said sincerely.

It really wasn't his intention to offend her by his questions, he just didn't realize the Humans still taught their young how to read. It wasn't as if it was something that could save their lives if it came to it. So, he just assumed it had died out like most things they used to do.

They walked in silence for a while before he finally asked: "If you don't mind me asking, how did you learn? Is it something you taught yourself?"

"No, my mother taught me when I was young."

Now he seemed to have upset her, yet he didn't know how. All he did was ask a question. It didn't seem to matter what he did or said, Taredd was always be putting his foot in it with her. She was either pissed off with him, or upset over something he said.

"I'm sorry if I've upset you," he told her.

"You haven't."

"Do you want to talk about it?"

Why the hell did I ask that?

Natalia captivated him in a way no other Human

ever had, and it confused the hell out of him. Normally he wouldn't give a shit about their feelings, but with Natalia it was different…he was different.

One thing was for sure, he really didn't like seeing her upset. He would rather her be pissed off and giving him grief, than quiet and withdrawn.

"What? Talk to you about my personal life? I don't think so," she said.

"Why not me?"

"Because you're probably the reason my mother isn't here anymore, that's why," she said angrily.

"She was killed?"

"Yes, Sherlock, she was. Now can you drop it?"

"I'm sorry for your loss," he said sincerely.

Natalia turned to look at him. He didn't know what she was looking for, but whatever it was she must have found it because she said: "Thank you."

"I'm not the only hunter around, you know." He didn't know why he needed her to know that, but he did. "So, it's quite possible someone else killed her."

"Really? You're not going to drop it, are you?"

That did seem to be the case. For some reason, he wanted to learn more about her. Plus, he was enjoying their conversation. It was completely different from the ones he had with Arun and Dain.

"No, I'm not," he admitted.

"Fine," she said, giving in to him. "One day she went out looking for food and she never came back."

"So, how do you know she's dead?" he asked. "She could have just left."

"No, she wouldn't have just left me," she said

adamantly.

"Why not?"

"Because she loved me, that's why," she told him. "You don't leave the people you love."

"I understand," Taredd had a feeling she wasn't telling him everything, but he didn't question her more about it.

"Do you?" she asked sceptically.

"Yes."

"What about you?" she asked after a moment's silence.

"What about me?"

"Do you have a mother?"

"Of course." Taredd laughed, he couldn't help it. "Everyone has a mother at one point in their lives. How else do you think I was born?"

"From an egg?"

"What? Did you think that an egg just fell out of the sky and I popped out of it?" he asked.

"Well, no," she said, looking at her feet. "I just thought you were created a different way."

The blush that crept up Natalia's face told him that she was embarrassed by her comment.

"What other way is there to create life?" he asked.

"I don't know. To be honest, I can't say I've really thought too much about it. After all, it wasn't a priority to know where you came from," she said. "We were too busy trying to stay away from you so we could stay alive longer."

"You keep saying we," he pointed out. "Were there more people with you other than just your mother?"

"Wouldn't you like to know," she said. "I'm not going to tell you anything you can use against my kind. So, you might as well save your breath."

"I wasn't trying to pry," he said innocently. "I was just curious, that's all."

"Yeah, I know why you're curious," she told him. "But I'm telling you now, I'm not going to give away anything about my kind, so you can just forget about it."

"That's not what I was after. I was just trying to get to know you a little better." Which was true.

Taredd didn't have a clue why he wanted to learn all about her when he'd never wanted to know anything about the Humans he'd come across before, but he did. There was something about her that intrigued him.

"Why?" she asked, tilting her head to one side as she looked up at him.

In that pose, she looked rather cute. Taredd didn't think she would appreciate him telling her that though, so he kept it to himself.

"Because I do."

"That's not an answer," she told him.

"Yes, it is."

"No, it's not," she countered.

"Well, it's the truth whether you believe it or not."

"Well, I don't."

"That's your choice. There's nothing I can say, or do, that will change your mind, is there?" he asked, knowing what the answer was going to be before she answered.

"Not really, no," she said.

Which was exactly what he thought she was going to say.

"See?" he said. "So why should I bother trying to prove to you that I don't have an ulterior motive?"

Instead of answering his question, she asked one of her own. "Are you like this with all of my kind?"

"No."

"So, why the interest in me?"

"I don't know," he said honestly. "You just intrigue me and I want to know more about you, is that so hard for you to believe?"

"Yes."

It was his turn to ask "Why?"

"Because, I'm nothing special," she was pensive. "So, why me?"

"I already told you," he said. "But you didn't accept my answer."

Taredd didn't know what more she wanted from him. He already told her he didn't know why she intrigued him, she just did. He felt compelled to learn all he could about her, and each moment that passed in her company, made him want to know even more.

CHAPTER SEVENTEEN

Natalia

Natalia really didn't understand this Demon. Why was he so interested in her? He admitted that he wasn't like it with any others of her kind, so why her? What made her so different from the rest of her kind?

Whatever the reason, Natalia wasn't about to complain. At the end of the day, as long as he kept his word and didn't kill her, then she couldn't give a shit about the whys. That was all that really mattered, after all. She couldn't find her way back to Amberly and Donovan if she was dead. So, unless she found a way to escape, she was going to have to take his word for it that she wasn't going to die.

"Are you hungry?" he suddenly asked out of the blue.

"What?" she asked, unsure if she heard right.

"Do you want something to eat?" he asked.

"Urm..."

"It's a simple yes or no answer," he said. "You're either hungry or you're not, so which is it?"

"Yes, I'm hungry," she said.

Her stomach rumbled and her mouth watered at the

thought of food. Because she had been too worried to eat more than a couple of bites since she arrived at the bunker, she was absolutely starving now.

"Do you have anything in that bag of yours?" he asked, pointing at her satchel. "Or do you need me to catch something?"

Natalia looked down at her satchel trying to remember if she put any food in it before they left, but unfortunately she hadn't. Natalia hadn't been thinking about food when she grabbed her stuff. It didn't help having a Demon watching her every move.

"Urm, I don't have anything left in there to eat," she told him. "And it's a satchel, not a bag."

"I stand corrected," he said. "Now, do you have a preference on what to eat? Or will anything do?"

"It depends, what do you mean by anything," she said, looking at him suspiciously.

"Rabbit?" he asked.

"Yeah, I suppose that'll do," she nodded.

"Good. Come with me," he said, waving for her to follow.

It wasn't as if she had a choice in the matter, she knew Taredd wouldn't let her stay behind because she could use that time to escape. So she couldn't stay behind even if she wanted to.

"Fine, if you insist," she said sarcastically as she followed him.

"Do you know how to catch a rabbit?" he asked.

"I can't say that I do," she said honestly.

In fact, Natalia didn't have clue how to catch anything. She'd never needed to know because she was always able to scavenge what she needed from the monsters.

"What do you know how to catch?" he asked.

"Nothing." She could have lied, but was there really any point?

His head snapped in her direction as he asked: "Really?"

"Yes, really," she said. "I've never needed to catch anything."

"So, what do you eat then?" he asked.

"Whatever we can scavenge," she said, shrugging her shoulder.

"Really?" he asked in disbelief. "So, you don't hunt your own food?"

"Nope."

"Where do you scavenge your food from then?" he asked.

Natalia wasn't sure how much to tell him. She didn't want it getting out to the monsters that they stole their food from them. If they found out the truth, then it wouldn't be so easy for her kind to steal from them anymore. Not that it was easy anyway.

"We just find what we can, wherever we can,," she told him instead of going into too much detail.

"I'm impressed you've made it this long then," he told her.

"Why?"

"Because that can't be an easy way to live," he said, shaking his head. "Not knowing where or when your next meal is coming? It must be hard."

"Life is hard," she said.

"But it doesn't have to be."

"For you, maybe. But have you forgotten who you're talking to?" she asked. "Since the day I was born life has been hard, it's nothing new to me. You may have had a better life, but not all of us are born with the same privileges as you. Some of us are born into a world that wants to ruthlessly hunt you down and kill you."

"I'm sorry," he said, surprising her.

"For what?" she asked, confused by his empathy.

"I'm sorry you had such a hard life."

"You say 'had' as if it's all in the past," she pointed out. "Nothing is in the past, it's still very much the present for me."

Thankfully, Taredd didn't say anything more about it after that. Instead, he set about making a trap, staying to the side out of her way so she could watch what he was doing. He was teaching her how to catch her own food, and she appreciated him doing that for her.

Natalia didn't ask him any questions, she just watched silently, taking in every detail she could. If she made it through… whatever this was they were doing together… alive and then managed to find Amberly, Donovan, and the rest of the group, she swore she was going to teach all of them how to do this as well.

Then they wouldn't need to reply on stealing from the monsters so much. They wouldn't have to risk their lives every time they needed to find food by getting so close to the monsters that were hunting them. It would mean that children wouldn't have their parents taken from them too soon, and parents wouldn't have their children taken from them either.

Once the trap was set, Taredd moved her away, saying it was better to leave it for a few hours before returning to see what they had caught.

"This will do," he told her when they came to a small clearing among the trees.

"This will do for what?" she asked, concerned she wasn't going to like the answer.

But he surprised her again by saying: "You said you needed a lot of sleep, so we'll camp here for tonight. Is that okay?"

Natalia looked around at the small clearing. It was already pitch-black outside when they had left the bunker, so she couldn't see the area very well, but it appeared to be okay. She still didn't know why they couldn't have just stayed in the bunker. They hadn't even travelled that far away from it either, so what gives?

"I thought you wanted to travel all night, wasn't that why we left the bunker?" she asked, confused.

"That was going to be the plan, until you said about sleeping every night and zombies," he said, with that irresistible smile of his on his face.

"Okay, so why did we leave the bunker then?" she asked. "There was plenty of beds there that we could have slept on."

"It was a hole in the ground," he stated as if that was a good enough answer.

"Yeah, with comfy beds," she countered.

"But it was still a hole in the ground."

"Yeah, I know," she agreed. "But it doesn't matter how many times you say that, it still has beds."

"I'm sorry, but no," he said with a disgusted look on his face. "I don't know how the fuck you ever stayed in one of those places. I couldn't wait to get out of the place before I even stepped foot in there."

"You get used to it," she told him.

"I agree, a bed would be nice, but not if it means sleeping underground," he said adamantly.

"You know, for a Demon, you really are fussy," she told him.

"And you know many Demons, do you?" he asked with a raised brow.

"Okay, you have me there," she admitted. "Apart from you, thankfully, I don't know any."

"You say thankfully as if it's a good thing," he said.

"Seriously? How do you keep forgetting who you're talking to?" she asked. "So, yes, I am very thankful."

"I'm sorry," he told her.

"Why do you keep apologizing to me as well?" she asked. "I'm the bloody captive, for fuck sake."

Taredd didn't reply. In fact, he didn't say another word at all, and neither did she.

Grateful for the silence, it gave Natalia time to think over the time they have spent together so far. The more time she was spending with him, the more he confused the hell out of her.

She could understand why he wouldn't want to stay in a hole in the ground, but the bunker wasn't just a hole. It was where she had spent her entire life.

Moving from place to place, it was always the same sort of accommodation. It was always a bunker buried deep beneath the ground.

It was the safest place for her kind. It wasn't that they hadn't tried to live elsewhere, because they had. Every time they did stay anywhere other than the bunkers, they had risked being caught. Even when they had no choice but to stop for the night as they moved between places, they couldn't let their guard down. One person had to be on watch at all times just in case they were spotted by the monsters.

But then, she didn't expect a Demon to understand any of that. It wasn't like they were hunted down and killed for no reason.

"Why do you kill my kind?" she suddenly blurted out.

Natalia hadn't intended to ask him that, but now it was out she really wanted to know the answer.

"What?" he asked.

"You heard me," she said. "Why do you hunt my kind? What have we ever done to deserve to be hunted down and murdered?"

Taredd just looked at her. If she didn't know better, she would say he was at a loss for words. Maybe he didn't want to upset her again? But that couldn't be right, why would it matter to him if she was upset or not? There must be some reason though, otherwise he wouldn't be staying silent right now. She already knew he killed her kind, so why wouldn't he tell her the reasons why he did it?

Instead of answering her question, he said: "Come

on, let's go and check on the trap."

Before she could say another word, he stood up and started walking away. Climbing to her feet, she raced after him. Natalia knew she should be running the other way, especially since he didn't look back to see if she was still with him or not. But she had to admit, she was intrigued to see if the trap worked.

It was exciting to think she might have caught her first ever meal. Well, technically it was Taredd that would have caught it, but still, she had been there as well.

CHAPTER EIGHTEEN

Taredd

It seemed that no matter how hard he tried not to, he was continuously putting his foot in it with Natalia. He would understand if he did actually keep forgetting that she was a Human, but he didn't, so he couldn't use it as an excuse. He just didn't appear to be able to think before he spoke while he was around her.

Taredd was coming to the conclusion that it was Natalia herself. She was the reason he wasn't himself at the moment. Maybe she was part Witch and had cast a spell on him.

That could explain why she didn't act anything at all like the other Humans he had come across so far. It was the only explanation he could come up with as to why he was acting so out of sorts.

The sooner they reach the others, the better. If she had such a strong effect on him in the short amount of time they have been together, then Taredd dreaded to think what it would be like if he spent an extended period of time with her.

It was a shame she needed to sleep every night, because if they didn't have to stop so often, then they could have caught up with Arun and Dain a hell of a lot sooner. As it was, they were going to be lucky if they caught up with them within a week.

At this rate, it was going to be closer to two weeks, if not more. To top it all, she wasn't the fastest at walking either, which really wasn't helping. Even now he had to slow his pace so she could keep up with him.

Taredd hoped that when she was finally asleep, he could put some space between them physically. If whatever it was that was wrong with him had anything to do with being in close proximity to her, then putting some space between them might be all that was needed for him to pull himself back together.

But first, he needed to be certain that she was fast asleep, otherwise she might take his absence as the perfect opportunity to escape. Hopefully he could at least get his shit together enough for them to reach Arun and Dain.

Taredd didn't know what was going to happen after that. He promised Natalia that she wouldn't die, but if he let her go, someone else might come along and finish her off. If that happened, he would have broken his promise.

The thought of someone killing her angered Taredd more than he expected, and definitely more than it should have. Not willing to look too deeply at why he had that reaction towards the thought of her death just yet, so he filed it away to look at later.

Mentally he shook his head to clear his thoughts and knelt down next to the trap to untangle the rabbit it caught.

"Have we caught something?" Natalia asked as she walked up behind him.

Even though Taredd told her to follow him, he'd completely forgotten to check if she actually was or not. To be honest, he was surprised to see she hadn't taken the opportunity to do a runner on him, but not as surprised as he was in the fact that she was actually taking an interest in what he was doing.

"Yes, we caught a rabbit," he told her.

"Wow, that was a lot quicker and easier than I thought it would be," she said. "I thought it might take all night before anything was caught."

"It depends where you set the traps. If you look..." he said, pointing at the ground around the trap. "... you can see the tracks are well worn, which indicates that it's used often, so it's the best place to set the trap."

He didn't know if Natalia could see what he was talking about. It was probably too dark for her to see the tracks, but she nodded her head all the same.

"I'll remember that for the future if..." she trailed off.

Taredd could tell she was about to say 'if I live long enough' at the end, but she didn't. So, for once, he managed to keep his mouth shut, instead of putting his foot in it like he was prone to do with her.

It amazed Taredd how he had gone from wanting to hunt down and kill every last Human being, to wanting one of them to live in the space of a few hours. And not just any one, but this one... Natalia. He didn't want to think what he was going to be like after spending a couple of days alone with her.

Once the rabbit was untangled and the trap cleared

away, he picked the animal up by the ears and carried it back to the camp. Taredd collected large sticks and logs along the way, while Natalia picked up twigs.

Dumping the sticks and logs in a pile in the middle of the clearing, Taredd hung the rabbit from a tree while he set about starting the fire. As soon as it was going, Taredd grabbed the rabbit again to skin and gut it before placing it over the fire. Before long, the animal was roasting nicely over the open flames.

Taredd sat back and relaxed, watching the flames dance as he waited for the meat to cook. The entire time he had been working, Natalia hadn't once taken her eyes off him. She watched intently as he prepared the animal and got the fire going.

Taredd assumed this was the first time she'd seen an animal be skinned, especially since she admitted she normally scavenged for food instead of catching her own. It didn't bother him that she watched him so closely. In fact, he rather liked the idea that he was teaching her something useful, something she could do for herself in the future.

He wanted to ask her more about how she scavenged food, but he didn't think she would appreciate more questions thrown her way. Not that she hadn't thrown her fair share of questions his way, but still, she didn't keep putting her foot in it like he did. Not only that, but he had a feeling he already knew the answer anyway.

Natalia hadn't spoken a word since they collected the animal from the trap. Every time he had peeked back at her while they were walking, to see if she was still with him, she had looked deep in thought. Even when she watched him work, she was deep in thought. He could tell that she had a lot on her mind, and it had nothing to do with what he had been doing.

So, instead of disturbing her with unnecessary questions, he sat quietly watching the flames. Consumed by a myriad of thoughts and feelings all of his own, he tried to make sense of them as they swirled around inside him.

CHAPTER NINETEEN

Natalia

Natalia was amazed at how fast Taredd had skinned and prepared the rabbit. It was the same with the fire as well., In a matter of minutes it was a roaring fire, warming her and shedding some light on the area.

Natalia wasn't complaining. No, she was more than grateful for his speed because she was absolutely starving, plus it was so cold she was finding it hard not to shiver.

So, if it meant she could warm up, even just a little bit, and fill her stomach to stop it from rumbling, then she definitely wasn't complaining. Natalia would have preferred it if he had gone a little slower though, so that she could see what he was doing, but she got the gist of it anyway.

If it had been left for her to do, then she would probably still be trying to figure it out. Natalia knew how to get a fire going, but it still took her at least twice as long as it had taken Taredd.

It was mesmerizing watching him work, especially once the fire was going and she could actually see what he was doing clearly. Luckily for her, Taredd had waited until he had the fire going before he started to skin the rabbit, otherwise she would still have no clue what to do with one.

What Natalia hadn't been expecting though, was for the rabbit to taste so good once it was finally cooked. When she had told him earlier that she didn't mind what he caught for dinner, she didn't want to mention to him that she's never tried rabbit before. At least, not that she had known about anyway.

As soon as she took the first bite she instantly knew she'd never eaten it before. Nothing she'd eaten had ever tasted so good, it almost melted in her mouth.

Natalia was definitely going to be eating it again. Especially since she knew how to catch it for herself now. It meant she wouldn't have to rely on scavenging so much. It was a lot nicer, and a hell of a lot safer, than scavenging from the monsters all the time.

If only she had known sooner how easy it was to catch the furry little creatures, she would have done it years ago. It would have saved so many lives over the years... maybe even her mother's.

That was all in the past now, Natalia couldn't do anything to change the past, but maybe she could change the future if she survived long enough.

Natalia tried her hardest not to look back, there was nothing but heartache and pain to be had from dwelling on things she couldn't change. So instead, she concentrated on the future instead, or at least tried to.

"Do you like it?" Taredd asked her out of the blue.

Natalia had been so caught up in her thoughts that she jumped when he spoke.

She looked up at him and then back at her food before saying: "It's really nice."

"You sound surprised," he said, smiling.

"To be honest," she said. "I wasn't expecting it to taste anywhere near as good as it does."

Smiling at her reply, he said: "So, does that mean this is going to be on the menu from now on?"

"If it's as easy for me to catch them as it was for you, then yes, they'll definitely be on the menu from now on."

"Good, I'm glad you're enjoying it," he said. "And I promise, it's that easy for everyone, you just need to find the perfect spot to set the trap."

"I hope you're right," she said.

"I am," he assured her.

Natalia was going to take his word for it. She couldn't wait to try it out for herself, she just hoped she lived long enough to be able to try it on her own.

She was even more eager to show Amberly and Donovan, but it was impossible at the moment. Until she could get away from Taredd, she had no chance in showing them or any of the others in their group.

Just because he promised not to kill her, it didn't mean he was going to share the same courtesy for the rest of her group. There was no way she would willingly risk the lives of everyone in the group, but especially not Amberly's and Donovan's lives.

Thinking about them made her heart ache. She longed to be back with them again. From as long as she could remember, this was the longest she had been separated from either of them. A small part of her even missed Bella, with her whiny voice and constant bitching.

Natalia wished she could at least check on them to make sure that they were safe and well. She wanted to let them know that she was okay, because she knew they would be just as worried about her as she was about them. She was beginning to feel more than a little homesick.

Mentally she shook her head to clear it from the negative thoughts. Then she said: "Thank you for catching and cooking this for me."

"You're welcome, Natalia," he said. " I couldn't let you starve to death now, could I."

Well, technically he could, but it would be breaking his promise to her.

She didn't want to point that out to him, so she said: "Well, thanks anyway."

Taredd nodded. "Have you had enough?"

"Yes, thank you."

"If you haven't, I can sort something else out for you to eat," he offered.

"No, seriously, I've had plenty now," she told him. "I'm going to try get some sleep now, that's if you don't mind?"

"Of course, you can," he said. "Why would I mind?"

"I don't know," she shrugged. "I just wanted to check, is all."

"Well, feel free to sleep whenever you're ready," he told her.

"Thank you."

"You don't have to thank me for that," he said.

"After all, that's why we've stopped for the night."

True, but Natalia couldn't help saying 'thank you' anyway. Her mother had taught her to always be polite, so it was ingrained in her to say 'please' and 'thank you', even if it was to a Demon.

Laying down facing towards the fire, Natalia watched Taredd for a moment before closing her eyes and throwing her arm over her face, trying to block out the light from the fire. When that didn't work as planned, she turned over and faced the other way.

Even without looking Natalia could feel Taredd's eyes burning a hole in the back of her head. Hopefully it wouldn't be long before he fell asleep, and that's when she was going to make her move.

If Natalia stood any chance in escaping, then she needed every advantage she could get.

CHAPTER TWENTY

Taredd

Relaxing against a tree Taredd watched Natalia, waiting for her to fall asleep. When her breathing evened out, he leaned his head back and closed his eyes.

His kind didn't need as much sleep as hers did, but he still enjoyed closing his eyes and listening to the sounds around him. What he hadn't expected, was to hear the sound of snapping twigs a short while later.

Taredd opened his eyes in time to see Natalia sneaking off.

"Where do you think you're going?" he asked, making her jump.

"Urm…I'm…urm…just going to the toilet," she stuttered.

"Over there will do," he said, pointing to a bush.

Natalia raised her eyebrows but didn't complain as she shuffled over to the bush.

He knew it wasn't what she originally had planned, he wasn't that stupid. She was trying to escape while he was asleep, at least, that's what she thought she was going to be doing.

Her shoulders were slumped when she walked back from the bush.

"Night," she said, laying back down in the same place as before.

Not trusting her to try sneaking off again, Taredd spent the rest of the night watching as she slept fitfully on the hard ground. Unfortunately there wasn't anything he could do about their sleeping arrangements tonight, but after watching her toss and turn he was going to make sure they had a proper bed tomorrow.

As much as he kept telling himself to put some distance between them physically, so that he could clear his head, he just couldn't bring himself to actually leave her. He could watch her to his hearts content and she wouldn't have a clue, not that he was content at all, far from it, in fact.

Taredd just couldn't seem to get enough of her. Her hair had a golden-brown appearance in the firelight. Her rosy lips and long thick black lashes stood out against her pale face.

Even though she tried to hide her body under tatty old clothes that were in serious need of washing, he could see her ample breasts and perfect curves. She was perfect in every way but one. She was Human, and he had to remember that.

As much as he wanted to wrap himself around her and hold her tight against his body, he couldn't. How could he when he had killed so many of her kind? How could he expect her to want anything from him, especially his touch, when he was holding her captive?

He couldn't. It was in both their best interests if he kept a tight hold of himself.

Whatever spell she had him wrapped up in, was digging its claws in deeper and deeper. He was worried if he spent too much more time around her, that whatever was wrong with him would be irreversible. But even knowing that, he still couldn't bring himself to leave her alone, just in case anything bad might happen. At least, that's what he kept telling himself anyway.

By the time he was finally ready to tear himself away from her, the sun had just started to rise. So much for pulling himself together while she slept. If anything, his feelings towards her had grown overnight, rather than diminish. He wasn't even sure if he was going to be able to leave her when they finally caught up with Arun and Dain, but it was looking less and less likely as time passed by.

He waited for the sun to fully rise before waking her, he didn't think she would appreciate being woken while it was still dark. He knew a Humans eyes weren't as good as his, so he knew Natalia would prefer to travel when she could see where she was going.

Gently nudging her, he said: "Natalia, Natalia, it's time to wake up."

"Five more minutes," she groaned, rolling away from him.

"Okay, but then you have to get up," he told her.

Groaning some more, Natalia said: "Fuck sake."

"What's the matter?" he asked her.

"Apart from being woken up by a Demon?" she asked.

"I wasn't sure if you remembered it was me or not with the way you asked for five more minutes," he admitted. "But I'm assuming I'm not the issue here. So, is there something else bothering you?"

"Oh, I didn't forget I was with you. I tried to... but I didn't forget," she said grumpily. "And yes, something else is bothering me."

"What is it? Can I help?" he asked.

"Not unless you have a soft mattress hidden somewhere," she said sarcastically. "Because these fucking sticks and stones have been digging into me all night."

"I'm sorry," he said. "But there's nothing I can do about that."

"Of course, there is," she snapped, sitting up to look at him.

"What could I have done?" he asked.

"You could have let me sleep in the bunker for one more night," she said. "But no, you wanted to leave straight away."

Taredd sighed. "I'm not going over this with you again. You'll never get me to stay in a hole in the ground."

"It's not a hole in the ground!" She snapped at him again. "It's a bunker. There's a difference, you know."

"Not as far as I can see, there isn't," he told her. But giving in a little, he added: "If you're that adamant about sleeping in a bed, I can arrange somewhere for us to stay tonight that isn't outside, but it does mean we have to leave sooner rather than later."

"So, in other words, get your ass up Natalia, because I've got a whole day of walking planned for you," she said, making her voice sound deep as she tried to imitate him. Then in her normal voice, she added: "Why, thank you, that sounds like loads of fun."

"Well, if you want to sleep in a bed tonight, then yes, we have a great distance to cover between now and then."

"Fine, I'll get up," she moaned.

"Not much of a morning person, are you?" As soon as the words left his mouth, Taredd wished he could take them back.

If looks could kill, Natalia would definitely have killed him with that one.

"Sorry," he said, holding his hands up and backing away in surrender.

Natalia didn't say a single word as she got herself up and ready to set off. She did, however, stomp around and giving him an evil look every time she glanced in his direction.

"Right, I'm ready to go," she said a short time later.

"Do you want anything to eat before we go?" he asked. "We have time if you do."

"No, I'm fine," she said. "Let's just get going."

"If you insist," he said.

Even biting off his head as soon as she opened her eyes didn't seem to alter his growing feelings for her. The fact she'd actually spent the night under the stars was more than he thought she would do. He knew it wasn't easy sleeping rough on the hard-unforgiving ground, so he was happy to take whatever she wanted to throw at him.

When he first mentioned sleeping rough, Taredd had imagined her getting up in the middle of the night and storming back to the bunker. He wouldn't have blamed her if she had because she had been right, they could have stayed there until the morning. It was only his stubborn refusal to stay underground that they didn't. They hadn't even travelled very far from the bunker before stopping for the night.

Taredd might have even gotten into her good books if they had, but at the time he didn't care about her feelings or staying on her good side. It amazed him at how quickly all that had changed. Now he wanted to be in her good books, he wanted to do anything in his power to make her happy.

Taredd followed behind Natalia, directing her when she drifted off course, but otherwise he didn't say a word to her. She didn't attempt to have a conversation with him either. She barely even acknowledged he was there half the time, so he assumed she wouldn't appreciate him trying to start one with her. Taredd didn't want to disturb her or piss her off more than she already had, but he wanted her to talk to him, he wanted to hear her voice.

They travelled like that for most of the day. Not once did she complain, or ask to stop for a rest. It was only when Taredd heard her stomach start to growl that he decided it was time for them to stop. He didn't care whether she wanted to or not, but he had a feeling she appreciated the break from walking.

Taredd didn't bother setting up a trap to catch a rabbit this time, mainly because he didn't plan on stopping for that long, but not only for that reason. Since they were right next to a river, he opted for catching a fish instead.

Natalia found a spot along the shore where she could sit and watch him fish. He didn't mind her watching what he was doing, because as long as her attention was focused on him, she wasn't looking for an escape route. But still, as he waded into the water he made sure to keep her in his sights at all times.

Staying as still as possible, Taredd waited patiently for a fish to swim between his submerged legs. Luckily for them, the river was teaming with fish, so it didn't take long for one to brush between his hands. Clamping his hands around the fish, he swiftly lifted it out of the water and then threw it on to the shore, right next to Natalia.

As soon as it landed next to her, she squealed as she jumped up and away from it. Taredd couldn't help but laugh. He hadn't known she would react in such a way when he threw it, but he had to admit, he might still have thrown it just to see how she would have reacted. And it would have been so worth it.

"Not funny," she said, pointing her finger at him. "You could have told me you were going to do that."

"What would you have done differently if you had known?" he asked.

"Well, I would have moved further away for starters."

Taredd wasn't sure if he should mention that it didn't

matter if she was further away, he would have still been able to throw it next to her, so he kept it to himself.

Taredd replaced his hands in the water so he could catch another one. This time he didn't throw it to the shore, he carried it out of the water instead, and made his way over to where Natalia was currently standing. He bent down and picked up the other fish as he walked passed where it landed, still flopping around on the ground.

As he reached Natalia side, he said "I hope you like fish."

"If it's anything like the rabbit, then I probably do."

"You've not even tried fish before?" he asked in surprise.

"Nope," she said, shaking her head as she smiled. "We tried to catch one once, but all we got was soaking wet."

Taredd had never seen Natalia smile before, but that wasn't what halted him. No, that was all down to Natalia's laugh. The sound was so magical it ensnared him instantly. Taredd wanted to hear more of it, so he swore… to himself at least… to make her laugh more often. Taredd didn't know how he was going to accomplish that feat, but he was definitely going to give it his best shot.

When she noticed him staring at her, she suddenly stopped laughing. He instantly missed the sound, and hated the fact it was because of him that she stopped.

"What?" she asked.

When he didn't reply straight away, she started

looking behind and all around her.

"What is it?" she asked again.

"Nothing," he finally said.

"Then why were you staring at me like that?"

"Sorry, it's just..."

"What?"

"Nothing," he said again, shaking his head. "Just forget about it."

"I don't want to forget about it," she told him, placing her hands on her hips. "I want to know why you were staring at me like that."

Taredd didn't say a word. He just walked passed her and headed towards the trees, so he could collect some firewood.

"I'm not going to give up, you know," she said, following hot on his heels. "You look as if you've seen a ghost or something."

Spinning around to see the look on her face as he admitted: "Because I liked the sound, okay?"

"Oh..." she said.

"Happy now?" he asked. "Does knowing that a Demon likes the sound of a human laughing make you happy?"

When she didn't reply, just stood there staring at him, he spun back around and stormed off towards the trees.

CHAPTER TWENTY-ONE

Natalia

The more time that Natalia spent with Taredd, the more she was becoming confused by him. She didn't have a clue what his problem was with her laughing. So what if he enjoyed the sound? It didn't bother her if he did like the sound, even if she didn't understand why.

Natalia had never liked her laugh, she thought it sounded stupid. So, for someone to say they enjoyed the sound, it was a complete first for her. Never in her wildest dreams did she think it would be a Demon though. Then again, she never thought she would spend this much time with a Demon and still be alive to talk about it.

Natalia had to admit, she was amazed he hadn't changed his mind about killing her this morning after she bit his head off. She knew it wasn't the wisest idea to piss him off, but she couldn't help herself.

Natalia wasn't a morning person at the best of times, but she was a bitch when she didn't get enough sleep and she knew it. After spending several nights camping out in freezing cold caves, Natalia was already in a crap mood.

Add in a shitty night's sleep on top of that because of the sticks and stones that dug into her while she slept, when she could have easily slept on a nice soft mattress. She had been pushed to the limits, so she was bound to let loose at the closest person to her.

Luckily enough for her, Taredd hadn't taken it the wrong way and didn't seem to be holding it against her.

She still wanted to know what his problem was though. She knew he was doing all this for a bet, but that still didn't explain why was he letting her live when he'd killed so many others of her kind.

She was positive just from looking at the size of him that he could have easily carried her dead body to wherever it was his friends were. He didn't need her to be alive to prove he won the bet, so why hadn't he?

It would have saved him a lot of hassle in the long run. So, what made her so different from the rest that he not only promised that she wouldn't die, but he actively went out of his way to make sure she had plenty of food and rest as well? It didn't make sense... he didn't make sense.

If Natalia was to believe every word he had said, then he would be providing her with a safe and comfy place to stay tonight as well. She didn't know if he was doing it for her benefit or his, but she was grateful either way. She wouldn't blame him if it was for his own benefit. After all, she was just a Human. A tiny insignificant speck in the grand scheme of things where he was concerned.

Sitting with her legs crossed in front of the fire, Natalia watched as Taredd cooked her yet another meal. Another new meal for her to try. She hadn't been paying close attention to how he caught the fish. After the first couple of minutes of watching him stand motionless in the water, Natalia had lost interest in what he was doing. Instead, she leaned back to look at the clouds in the sky.

Natalia knew she would never be able to stand as still as Taredd had done for long enough to catch anything that way. If there was an easier way to catch fish, then she was all for it. That's if it turned out any good, otherwise it would be a complete waste of time trying to find another way to catch them. If it tasted anything like the rabbit did last night, then she was definitely going to enjoy fish as well.

"Here you go," Taredd said, passing her one of the cooked fish.

"Thank you," she said as she accepted it.

It certainly didn't smell as good as the rabbit had done. For such a small thing, it had a very potent smell. Natalia just hoped it tasted better than it smelt. Especially if she was going to stand any chance in getting the others in the group to try it.

She knew without a doubt the others would want her to cook this meal outside of the bunker though, and she couldn't blame them, she wouldn't want the bunker stinking of fish either. It was hard enough keeping the bunker smelling fresh as it was, without adding to the problem. With it being deep underground, it wasn't like they could crack open a window or anything.

At least the rabbit didn't smell as bad as the fish. Natalia didn't think she would have a problem convincing the others to try the rabbit, but the fish? She was going to have a hard time convincing them to give it a try whether it tasted better than it smelt or not.

"Once you've finished, we'll get going again," he told her.

"Okay. Have we got much further to go today?" Natalia asked, trying to postpone eating the smelly fish.

Taredd didn't let the conversation stop him from eating though. He tucked right in, pulling it apart easily using his fingers.

"It should only take us a couple of hours to reach our destination," he told her between mouthfuls.

"Where is it that you're taking me?" she asked.

"There's a town not far from here, that's where we are heading," he said. "Are you going to eat that or what?"

Natalia didn't like the sound of that. Being in a town surrounded by monsters that wanted to kill her didn't seem like the best of ideas.

Even knowing there would be, Natalia couldn't help but ask: "Are there going to be Demons and other monsters there?"

"Yes, of course there will be others there, it wouldn't be a town otherwise, would it?" he told her. "Now, eat up so we can get going."

Natalia dubiously picked up a small piece of fish, she told him: "This better not taste disgusting."

Shaking his head at her, he didn't say a word, just

sat there smiling at her. Pulling a face at the smell, Natalia gingerly placed the piece of fish in her mouth. At first, she wasn't too keen on the taste, but after a moment she realized it was nowhere near as bad as it smelt. In fact, Natalia found that she really liked it.

Fish is definitely on the menu from now on as well, she thought as she vigorously tucked in.

Natalia knew Taredd was right about the town, it wouldn't be much of a town if there weren't any people… or monsters as the case may be… living there, but it didn't make it any easier on her. The more monsters around her, the higher the chance she had of being killed.

Reading her mind, he said: "Don't worry about the people in the town, I'll keep you safe."

"How do you plan on doing that?" she asked. "You can't watch me 24/7."

"Why can't I?" he asked.

"What? So, you're going to watch me the whole time we're there?" she asked sceptically. "You're not going to take your eyes off me for one second?"

"If I have to, then yes," he told her. "It shouldn't be necessary though. Once everybody sees that you are with me, they should leave you alone."

It didn't matter how much he tried to reassure her, she didn't have as much faith in the other monsters that he did. He was only one person… Demon… at the end of the day. As much as he told her he can keep an eye on her 24/7, he couldn't because it was impossible to watch someone that closely.

There were bound to be times when he wasn't

watching her, and it was in one of those times that the other monsters could take the opportunity to kill her. These were the moments she was most concerned about.

Natalia didn't bother saying anything more about it though. She didn't think it would matter what she said, he wasn't likely to change his mind on the matter. After all, she was his captive, so she didn't really have much of a choice but to do as he wanted.

"Everything will be fine," he told her again.

"Okay," she said, still not convinced but not willing to debate it anymore either.

"I promised you wouldn't die," he told her. "And I intend on keeping my promise."

Dusting off her hands when she couldn't bring herself to eat anymore, she said: "I'm ready to go."

The thought of being surrounded by a bunch of monsters had turned her stomach upside down. Completely putting her off the food. Luckily enough, Taredd didn't say another word about it. There wasn't much he could say to make her feel better about it. Only time would tell which one of them was going to be right. Natalia prayed it was going to be Taredd, but it was more than likely going to be her.

CHAPTER TWENTY-TWO

Taredd

Taredd knew she didn't believe he could keep her safe around the other 'monsters' as she called them, but there was no doubt in his mind.

Natalia may not know what he was capable of, but he knew what his abilities were and he knew he could keep her safe because of them. But there was only one way he could prove that to her though, and that was by taking her there and showing her.

Natalia hadn't said a word since they left the river, she didn't even look in his direction once. Taredd didn't know if he had done anything to upset her other than take her to the town, but he didn't want to piss her off more by asking either. So, he just walked next to her in silence.

As he told Natalia, it only took them a couple of hours to reach the town, even walking at Natalia's slower pace. Natalia didn't say a word to him until the small town came into view.

She turned to him, eyebrows pinched together with worry, she said: "I hope you're right about this."

"I am," he told her. "Nothing will happen to you

while you are in my care."

"Fine, but if you're wrong and I end up dead," she said, pointing a finger at him. "Then I'm gonna come back and haunt you for the rest of your life."

Taredd couldn't help but laugh. It wasn't that he didn't believe ghosts existed, because he knew they did. It was the way Natalia was threatening to come back and haunt him for the rest of his life that made him laugh.

He didn't know whether or not to divulge that he could interact with ghosts just like he did with the living. He didn't think she would appreciate that bit of information, so he kept it to himself.

"Okay," he said. "But it will not be necessary, because nothing is going to happen to you."

"We'll see," she told him, turning her back to him again.

"Yes, we will," he agreed.

Even though he was confident no one would bother her since she was with him, he still kept her close to him while they navigated the streets looking for a place to stay.

"In here," he said when they came to a tavern.

"Are you sure?" she asked, eying up the outside of the building.

"Very," he said confidently.

"If you say so," she said sceptically.

"Just... come on," he said as he held the door open for her.

She walked in without saying another word. He knew she wasn't happy to be here, but it was the closest place with a bed and somewhere for them to clean up.

Taredd scanned the street before walking in after her. It wasn't often a Human was seen walking around towns anymore, especially the smaller ones that were off the beaten track like this one. So he expected to garner some interest from the locals, and he wasn't disappointed.

A few people had stopped to watch them as they walked down the street and into the tavern, while others watched as they continued on their travels. Taredd wasn't concerned with any of them.

In fact, he was more concerned about the people that didn't seem to have any interest in them at all. If anyone was going to cause them any trouble while they were here, it was going to be those people and not the ones watching them.

Taredd had taken a note of each individual before he followed Natalia into the tavern.

"What took you so long?" Natalia whispered as he reached her side.

"Sorry, I thought I saw one of my friends," he lied.

There was no point telling her the truth, that he was looking for anyone who could possibly cause them any trouble, because otherwise she would definitely not believe that he could keep her safe. It would only cause him more problems in the long run. So, he kept it to himself.

"I take it, it wasn't your friend," she said, looking up at him.

"No, it wasn't him," he said. "Just someone that

looks similar."

"I'm sorry," she said.

Confused, he asked "Why?"

"Because if it had been your friend, then you could have proven to them that you've won the bet sooner," she said. "Then you wouldn't be stuck with me any longer."

"It's okay," he told her. "I'm sure we'll find them soon enough." Leading her over to the bar at the back of the room, he added "But for now, let's just see if we can get a room for the night and something to eat."

Taredd didn't mention he actually wanted her to stay with him for longer, a hell of a lot longer in fact. How much longer he didn't know, but he was slowly growing more attached to her the more time he spent with her.

"Sounds good to me," she said.

"Good, come on."

Natalia didn't say a word as she let him lead her over to the bar. Taredd noticed she was looking around the room at everyone in here. Nobody would start on her while he was with her, but he still wanted her to stay close to him. He didn't need to tell her though, because she was right on his heels the entire way.

A Shapeshifter stood behind the bar, watching them as they made their way over.

Greeting them with a smile, he said: "Evening, what can I get you?"

"Evening," Taredd replied politely. "Do you have a room available for the night?"

"For you... and the Human?" he asked with one eyebrow raised as he looked over at Natalia.

"Yes," Taredd replied curtly this time. "Do you have a problem with that? If so, I am more than happy to take my business elsewhere."

"Nope, it's fine by me," he said, shaking his head. "Just needing to be sure, but as long as you don't cause any problems, then the Human is welcome to stay with you."

"Good."

"Just the one room?"

"Yes, one will do. Thank you."

"Do you want something to eat or drink before I show you to your room?" he asked.

Taredd turned to Natalia in time to see her lick her lips at the mention of food.

Smiling, he turned back to the Shapeshifter and said "I think we'll have something to eat first."

After giving their food and drinks order, Taredd lead Natalia over to a table that was in the back of the room, tucked into the corner by an open fire.

"Thank you," Natalia said, taking a seat in the chair he pulled out for her.

"For what?"

"Not making me sit out in the open," she said, indicating the empty tables dotted around in the rest of the room.

It wasn't the reason why he picked this particular table, but he was happy to let her believe it was.

"You're welcome," he told her instead.

The real reason why he picked this spot was for the

view. It was a prime location to be able to see everyone in the room, as well as anyone that came and went. It was also the perfect position to prevent anybody from sneaking up on them from behind, so he didn't have to worry about looking backwards every two seconds.

There was even a reason why he held out a chair for Natalia to sit in, and it wasn't to be helpful or kind. It was so he had a completely uninterrupted view of the room.

As soon as they were seated, the Shapeshifter brought over their drinks, then disappeared into a back room to sort out their meal. It didn't take long before he returned with a tray of food for them.

"Thank you," Taredd told him as he placed the plates on the table in front of them.

"No problem," he replied. "Just shout if you want anything else."

Natalia picked up the spoon the Shapeshifter placed on the table for her, and started swirling it around in her bowl of food.

"It's not poisonous, you know," Taredd told her. "It's only food, and I promise it doesn't taste that bad."

"It doesn't look too nice though," she said, pulling a face at it.

"Try it," he encouraged. "You won't know if you like it if you don't try it."

"Fine, but if I get food poisoning, you'll be cleaning up the mess after I've projectile vomited everywhere," she said, waving her spoon at him.

"Okay, that's a deal," Taredd agreed.

"I'm not offering you a deal," she told him. "I'm stating a fact, because I'm seriously not cleaning up sick after being given food poisoning again."

"As I said, it's not a problem, because you're not going to get food poisoning," he said, shaking his head. "Now, stop playing with your food and eat up already."

"Fine, but don't say I didn't warn you," Natalia told him.

Admittedly, it didn't live up to his standards, but it didn't taste too bad, and it certainly wasn't going to give her food poisoning. Even still, Natalia sniffed the food and licked a little off the spoon before finally giving in and eating it properly.

Taredd couldn't help but smile... and be slightly turned on... when her tongue peeked out and licked the spoon. Whatever spell she had on him, was getting stronger by the minute. Taredd didn't know whether he should be worried or not, but for the time being, he was going to take each moment as it came.

CHAPTER TWENTY-THREE

Natalia

As much as Natalia didn't like the look of the sloppy food in the bowl, it didn't taste too bad. It reminded her of the fish she had eaten earlier that day, it smelt awful but tasted delicious.

The drink Taredd had ordered for her on the other hand, was absolutely heavenly. Natalia didn't have a clue what it was, and she didn't care either. It gave her a nice warm tingly feeling in her stomach, and a slightly fuzzy feeling to her head.

"See? I told you it wasn't poisoned," Taredd said, pointing towards her nearly empty bowl.

"Hey, it still could be poisonous, it might just take time to kick in," she told him. "I've had that happen before."

Taredd shook his head at her, but he had that cute smile back on his face again.

How can I find anything about him cute? He's a Demon for fuck sake!

It was really starting to confuse Natalia. She was supposed to fear his kind, and had done for all her life, but now she was finding it difficult not to be attracted to a Demon. Not just any Demon though, it was all for Taredd.

Looking around the room at all the other monsters, she didn't know if any of them were Demons like Taredd, but she knew for sure that none of them were anywhere near as attractive as he was. Which was a good thing, because being sexually attracted to one Demon was bad enough, especially since she should be as scared of him as she was with the rest of them.

Natalia mentally kicked herself. She needed to pull herself together if she was ever going to find a way to escape from him, because that was still her plan. She needed to get back to the others as quickly as possible. Her heart ached because she missed Amberly and Donovan so much.

Natalia didn't even know if they had made it through the pass alive. For all she knew, they could have frozen to death in one of the caves, or worse, they could be out looking for her. That was the last thing she wanted. It was too dangerous, especially if they found her tracks and followed them here.

Natalia got a sick feeling in the pit of her stomach at the thought of them following her here. They would have to sneak past an untold number of monsters just to reach the tavern. If they made it that far unseen, then they would definitely be seen as soon as they stepped foot inside the building.

She could imagine her friends being surround by a sea of monsters before they'd even had a chance to do so much as blink.

She wasn't only worried about the other monsters in

the room though. As much as Taredd had promised that she wouldn't die by his hand, he had made no such promise to her friends.

Admittedly, Taredd didn't know anything about her friends, but that was for their safety. Until she knew for sure that they were going to be safe around Taredd as she was, she couldn't say a word about them to him.

Natalia couldn't shake the worry from niggling away at the back of her mind that they have managed to get themselves caught by the monsters since she left them. She prayed that nothing bad had happened to them. It would hurt worse than it already did knowing that she wasn't around to help them.

Natalia lost her appetite. The thought of something bad happening to the rest of her group... to Amberly and Donovan in particular... twisted her stomach into knots.

Placing her spoon in the bowl, Natalia picked up her drink and downed the last of it. The tingly feeling spread deliciously through her body again. Surprisingly, it helped to ease the feelings that swirled around inside her, trying to consume her with thoughts of helplessness and grief.

"Have you finished?" Taredd asked, making her jump.

"Urm..," she said, looking between him and the half-eaten bowl. "... yeah... I've had enough... thank you."

"You're welcome," Taredd said. "I'll be finished in just a minute, then we can go up to our room if you're ready?"

"That's okay, you can take your time," she told him,

but he didn't listen.

Putting his spoon down on the table, Taredd then picked up the bowl and drank the last of its contents before doing the same with his drink.

"Come on, let's go," he said, putting the cup back on the table when he was finished.

"You didn't have to do that you know, I was quite happy to wait for you to finish," she told him honestly.

"I know," he said. "But I don't know about you, but I could do with some rest."

Natalia would have believed he was tired if he hadn't already told her he could stay awake for days on end. Natalia on the other hand, was drained physically and emotionally.

It amazed her how much it had tired her out just worrying about her friends… her family… so she was happy to let him keep his lie. She was happy for him to lead her to a bed where she could sleep and forget all about her worries, if only for a short while.

"I'm ready when you are," she told him.

Leaving their dirty dishes on the table, Natalia follow Taredd over to the bar before they followed the bartender through a door at the back of the room and up a flight of stairs. Natalia didn't say a word as she followed them down a hallway and into a room at the furthest end away from the stairs.

"Here you go." the bartender said as he held out something for Taredd.

Natalia couldn't see what it was, but she guessed it was a key as he used it to open the door when the bartender walked off, leaving them alone again.

Holding the door open for her, Taredd said: "As promised, a comfy bed for you for the night."

"Thank you," she said, walking into the room with Taredd hot on her heels.

The first thing she noticed, was the one large bed standing proud, smack bang in the middle of the room.

This is so not a good idea.

How the hell was she supposed to fight her attraction to him, when she was going to be sleeping in the same bed as him?

CHAPTER TWENTY-FOUR

Taredd

"Will this room do for you?" Taredd asked as he followed her into the room.

From the look on her face, he knew straight away that something was wrong with it.

"Yep, this will do nicely, thank you," Natalia said, looking around the room. "But there's only one bed, so where are you going to sleep? Do you have the room next door or something?"

"Nope, if I need to sleep, I will be sharing the bed with you," he told her.

"Urm, no, I don't think so," she said, shaking her head.

And there it was, the problem she had with the room, was the fact it only had the one bed. Before she even opened her mouth, Taredd knew it was because there was only one bed.

Admittedly, he should have known she wouldn't be happy about sharing the bed with him, but it honestly hadn't crossed his mind when he asked for one room that the Shapeshifter would give them a room with one bed in it.

Luckily enough for them, it was a king-sized bed, so they would both be able to fit on it without a struggle. Taredd's feet would end up hanging off the end, but there weren't many beds where that didn't happen to him.

"Urm, yes, I think so," he said, copying her as he nodded his head.

"There is no way in hell that I'm sleeping in a bed with you," she said adamantly.

"You're more than welcome to sleep on the floor if you would like?" he offered.

Natalia looked down at the wooden floor boards before looking back up at him. He could see from her face before she even opened her mouth that she wasn't going to go for that idea either.

"I don't think so buddy," she said, shaking her head. "If anyone is going to sleep on the floor, then it's definitely going to be you."

"But I paid for the room," he pointed out.

"I don't care," she said. "I'm still not sleeping in that bed with you."

"So, you would sleep in another bed with me then?" he asked jokingly.

Natalia stood staring at him for a moment with her mouth wide open.

When she finally stopped gaping at him, she said "That's not what I meant, and you know it wasn't."

Yeah, he did know she didn't mean it that way, but he couldn't help himself, it was amusing seeing her reaction to his comment.

"I am not sleeping on the floor, Natalia," he said

clearly.

"Well, you're not sleeping in the bed with me, Taredd."

Taredd was so taken aback by her saying his name that he stood motionless, staring at her for a moment while he tried to think of a comeback. It was the first time since he met her that she's called him by his name.

He hadn't expected to have such a reaction, but the way his name rolled off her tongue sent blood rushing straight to his cock.

Clearing his throat... and mentally shaking his head... he finally found his voice again.

"Well, it doesn't matter what you have to say," he told her. "It's happening that way whether you like it or not."

Taredd could tell Natalia wanted to argue with him, but she didn't. Instead, she huffed out a breath and stormed over to the bed, throwing her satchel down when she was next to it.

"Fine, but stay on your side of the bed," she said, glaring at him over her shoulder.

"I will try my best," he told her. "But just so you know, I do tend to fidget in my sleep."

"Yeah right," she said under her breath.

If Taredd's hearing hadn't been as heightened as it was, then he never would have heard it. But as it was, he heard her loud and clear.

Turning back to him, Natalia said "Just so you know, I have a habit of fighting in my sleep whenever I get to close to anyone."

Bullshit. Taredd thought before saying aloud: "Now you're just making shit up."

Putting her hands on her hips, she shook her head and said adamantly "No, I'm not."

"Natalia, I watched you sleeping last night," he told her. "I know for a fact that you don't fight in your sleep."

"Yeah, that's because I was sleeping on sticks and stones. I didn't want to move just in case it made it worse," she told him. Then pointing her finger at him, she added: "Plus, you weren't sleeping right next to me."

Taredd could tell she was making it up to try to deter him from sleeping next to her, but it wasn't working. He would wait until she was fast asleep if that made it any easier, but either way, he was sleeping in that bed whether she liked it or not. So, there was no point in arguing with her about it.

"How do you know I wasn't sleeping next to you?" he asked her. "You were snoring your head off most of the night, so for all you know, I could have been."

The look on Natalia's face was priceless. Taredd was finding it increasingly difficult not to burst out laughing, but then she would know he was talking bullshit, so he bit his tongue and kept a straight face.

When he couldn't take her evil glare any more, he finally gave in and lied to her and said: "Fine, I'll take the chair."

"Good," she said, turning her back to him once again. "Well, I don't know about you but I'm shattered, so I'm going to bed now."

Taredd took the opportunity to laugh silently while her back was to him, but as soon as she looked back at him, he composed himself swiftly enough that she didn't notice.

Natalia gave him a quizzical look, but didn't say anything as she pulled back the covers and sat on the side of the bed to kick off her shoes.

"That's fine by me," he told her.

The sooner she was asleep, the sooner he could climb into bed, because there was no way he was paying for a room with a bed he couldn't sleep in. Taredd walked over to the chair in front of the window. He scanned the area from his seat before returning his attention to the bed.

Natalia had taken off her coat, but left on her trousers and t-shirt, before she climbed into bed. She pulled the blankets up around her to just under her chin and settled down for the night. Taredd watched as Natalia settled down into a comfortable position.

Wishing he could just climb right into bed next to her, Taredd prayed it didn't take her long to fall asleep. It had been a few nights since he last slept, and the exhaustion was starting to catch up with him. Even if he only managed to get a couple of hours sleep tonight, it should be enough to help clear his mind.

Luckily for him, it wasn't too long before he heard her breathing even out as she drifted off. Taredd didn't jump up straight away, instead he waited a little longer, making sure she was definitely fast asleep before joining her. Then he stripped off quietly and gently climbed in bed next to her, being as careful as he could not to disturb her.

Resting his arms behind his head, Taredd instantly doubted his decision to strip bare while sleeping next to her. Maybe it wasn't the wisest of ideas he had had recently, but Taredd wasn't about to climb back out of bed again just so he could redress. Instead, he laid there looking up at the ceiling.

It wasn't long after Taredd got himself comfortable, that he regretted his decision even more. Without any encouragement on his part, Natalia rolled over and curled up right next to him, then let out a long-contented sigh.

Yep, definitely not a good idea. He thought as all the blood rushed south.

If she woke up right at this moment and realized that he was not only in bed with him, but completely naked and fully erect, she was likely to throw a fit. He could even imagine her trying to kick his naked ass out of bed, not that she would have much luck, he could easily overpower her without much effort. It still wasn't enough to make him reassess his decision.

Well, shit happens.

Because there was no way he was budging from this position, even if she did wake up. Plus, there wasn't much he could do about it now without disturbing her anyway, so he might as well get some sleep while he could. Tomorrow was going to be another long day.

CHAPTER TWENTY-FIVE

Natalia

Natalia should have known something like this was going to happen. It wasn't the first time, and it probably wouldn't be the last either.

At some point during the night, Natalia had stripped off all her clothing except a rather small pair of knickers and a small thin strappy vest top that barely covered her breasts.

She didn't know why she did this in her sleep, but she was thankful it only ever happened when she was sleeping in a bed. Maybe she got too hot during the night and that was why she had a tendency to strip.

What she definitely hadn't been expecting though, was to wake up with someone else in the bed with her. An extremely large... and extremely naked... Demon was laying right next to her. It wasn't just any Demon either, it was Taredd.

The one Demon in the whole entire world that she was attracted to, and that wasn't even the worst part about it. No, that was nowhere near as bad as what she came to realize next.

Taredd had one of his arms wrapped around her as

she cuddled up against him. In fact, she was so close to him that half of her body was sprawled over his, with one of her legs covering his manhood under the blankets. Which meant she couldn't move an inch without disturbing him.

How the hell do I manage to keep getting myself into situations I can't get back out of? She thought .

Natalia couldn't help blushing at where her leg was resting. It was right on top of a very large cock, which picked that exact moment to move, letting her know that it was also a fully erect cock as well. Natalia slowly looked up to see that Taredd was wide awake and looking right back at her.

Natalia froze as their eyes clashed. Her heart was racing so fast she could feel it thumping against him. It was beating so loudly in her ears that it drowned out all other sounds.

With a life all of its own, the leg she had covering his cock decided to rubbed against him. She watched as his eyes dilated with desire as he lifted his hips in return, pushing himself harder against her.

She kept telling herself that this was probably the worst idea in the world, but as much as she kept informing her body of this, apparently it had a completely different opinion on the matter. As the rest of her body took on a life of its own, joining in with her leg and rubbing up against him.

Without breaking eye contact, Taredd lowered his head towards hers. Stopping just millimetres away, giving her the perfect opportunity to put a stop to all this madness. But instead of pushing him away like she should have done, Natalia covered the rest of the distance, gently brushing her lips against his.

Taking her move as encouragement to go on, Taredd opened his mouth slightly and, with the lip of his tongue, he lightly licked along the seam of her lips. Taredd didn't waste any time, as soon as she opened her mouth for him, he took full advantage. Deepening the kiss, he devoured her mouth. Natalia couldn't help herself as she melted in his arms, met his fiery kiss with one just as fiery.

Natalia had been so engrossed with the magic of his mouth, she hadn't noticed that his other arm had moved until his hand gently caressed her face, brushing away the strands of hair that was getting in her face. When he was done brushing her hair out of the way, his hand slowly made its way down her body until it rested over her breast.

Natalia pushed out her chest when his hand stopped, trying to encourage him to do more. Taredd took the hint, gently stroking her nipple with his thumb over the thin fabric encasing them. Before long he was gently squeezing and plucking her nipple between his thumb and forefinger. Natalia moaned into his mouth as pleasure shot from her nipple to her core.

Even if she wanted to Natalia couldn't have stopped her body from moving now. It had completely taken on a life of its own, grinding against the side of him. So, since she had no intention of stopping, she decided to go with it, letting her body take the lead.

Natalia used her free hand to snake down his chest and stomach, heading straight for his rock-hard cock.

Taredd was a hell of a lot larger than any man she had ever been with before. Natalia couldn't get her fingers anywhere near each other as they encircled his cock, so she settled for just stroking it as best as she could.

Gently taking as much of him in her hand as she could fit, she began to slowly work her way up and down, circling the tip of his cock with her thumb each time she stroked up.

Taredd rolled Natalia onto her back. Before she had a chance to protest as he made her break contact with his cock, he rolled half on top of her with one of his legs wedged between hers, spreading them with his knee so he had access to the most vulnerable part of her.

Lifting her small vest top over her breasts, exposing more of her to his touch, Taredd broke the kiss so he could take her peaked nipples into his mouth. Natalia couldn't help pushing her chest up into his mouth.

She could feel the moisture building between her legs as he lavished her breasts with attention. Moving from one to the other, he paid them both the same amount of attention before moving further down her body.

Kissing her bare skin along his way, Taredd didn't stop until he reached her core. Spreading her legs as wide as they would go, he leaned back and took in the sight of her. She could just imagine how wet it looked to him, she could feel the moisture as it continued to gather there.

Licking his lips, he looked up at her with desire swimming in his eyes and growled huskily, "Mine."

Then, he leaned in to devour her.

Natalia bucked against his face as his tongue made contact with the bundle of nerves between her legs for the first time. She was by no means a virgin, but not a single person had ever licked her there before, so she hadn't been prepared for the exquisite pleasure that shot straight through her body, making her gasp before letting out a long moan of pleasure.

Tentatively, Natalia reached down and gently touched the tip of his horns. She didn't know what she expected to happen when she touched them, but it certainly wasn't the pleasure filled groan that came from him, the sound vibrated against the bundle of nerves which in turn made her moan.

Encouraged by Taredd's reaction, Natalia gently touched them again before wrapping her hands around each horn and rubbing them in unison, like she had been doing with his cock before he changed position, preventing her from being able to reach.

Natalia couldn't stop her body from gyrating against his face, as much as she tried to keep still for him, she couldn't. Her body was completely out of control. It didn't seem to faze Taredd though, if anything, her movements seemed to spur him on more.

Natalia didn't know how much more of it she could take without exploding, she was barely hanging on to the cliff edge as it was, and it appeared that he had no intention of stopping any time soon.

Grabbing hold of both of her thighs, Taredd lifted them into the air. When he was satisfied, she wasn't going to lower them again, he let go of one leg. It didn't take long for Natalia to realize why.

She sucked in a breath as the tip of one of his fingers circled round the entrance to her core. All the while, he continued lavishing attention to the bundle of nerves just above where his finger was circling.

Natalia lifted up her hips, wanting more. Taredd gave her exactly what she wanted, he slowly and gently slid his finger into her moist core. When his finger was as far as it could go inside of her, he twirled it around before pulling it all the way out again.

He repeated the slow torturous movement several times before speeding up. Natalia found herself rocking her hips in time with the motion of his finger. As his hand sped up, so did his tongue. She was being bombarded by sensations.

When Taredd added a second finger, Natalia bucked off the bed as her orgasm washed over her. Taredd didn't stop sliding his fingers in and out of her, even when she was finally spent and laying limp on the bed, he continued to pump his fingers.

Taredd lifted his head to look up at her and said in a husky voice: "So fucking sexy."

CHAPTER TWENTY-SIX

Taredd

Taredd couldn't believe what he and Natalia were doing. It was the last thing in the world he expected to happen when she first woke up and realized he was in bed with her. But he also hadn't expected her to strip down to her underwear either.

If it wasn't for the thin bits of fabric covering her perfect breasts and pussy, then she would be as naked as he was.

He didn't have a clue how or when that happened, but he certainly wasn't going to complain about it. Especially not when his face was currently buried between those beautiful legs of her, feasting on the juices gathering there.

Taredd hadn't bothered to remove her last remaining clothing, he just moved them out of the way so he had easy access to what he wanted to play with.

Natalia bucked uncontrollably underneath him, as he continued to flick his tongue as fast as he could against the bundle of nerves. He did it a few more times before he slid his tongue down to the entrance of her pussy and flicked it in and out of her slick walls.

Her taste was addictive to him, it was like the sweetest ambrosia he has ever had in his extremely long life. And the way her body came to life for him with the slightest of touches, made his cock pulse with anticipation.

He couldn't wait to slid his cock deep inside of her. Taredd knew she was wet enough for him to slide in easily, but first he needed to prepare her a bit more so she was ready to take the size and width of him. Plus, he wanted more of her taste in his mouth.

So, he had to settle for using his fingers for the time being. Moving his mouth back to her pussy, Taredd continue to fuck her with two of his fingers until he was sure she could take another one. They glided in and out without a problem, her pussy was dripping wet, making it easy for him. hips rocking with the motion of his hand.

Natalia was so hot and wet for him that he found it hard not to just slam his cock into her pussy to the hilt. He craved to be in her more than he wanted to take his next breath, but he had to be patient, he needed to make sure she was prepared to take him. The last thing Taredd wanted to do to her, was to hurt her because he hadn't prepared her enough to take his large cock.

When she was ready and begging for more, Taredd ignored her protests as he slowed the pace of his hand down. She instantly stopped complaining as he gently squeezed in a third. By the time he slid in a fourth finger Natalia was going wild on the bed, pushing against him at the same time as trying to move away. So, using his other hand, Taredd pinned her in place.

Taredd continued to devour her pussy with his mouth and tongue as he pumped his fingers in and out, slowly at first until she was accustomed to the thickness of them together. Only once she was able to take all four easily, and she had stopped trying to move away from his hand, did he finally pick up the speed again.

Throwing her head from side to side, Natalia was panting as the pleasure built up to tipping point again. Taredd could feel the walls of her pussy squeezing his fingers. Before he let her tip over the edge again, he sat back and watched the play of emotions on her face as he fucked her with his fingers.

"So beautiful," he told her. "So fucking beautiful."

Her breasts bounced as she rode his hand, and a rosy sheen had covered her skin. Taredd couldn't wait any longer, he wanted - needed - to be buried to the hilt inside of her pussy right this instant.

Natalia groaned in protest again when he pulled his fingers out, but as he lined up his cock with her pussy and nudged her entrance with the tip she sucked in a breath in anticipation. He didn't make her wait, because he couldn't wait any longer himself.

Grabbing hold of her by the hips, Taredd lifted her up slightly so he had better access, and slid the tip of his cock inside her. Natalia bit her bottom lip as he breached her entrance as slowly as he could. She was so hot and wet, enticing him to push in further, which he eagerly did.

"Fuck," he bit out between clenched teeth.

Natalia moaned as he slowly pushed his cock inch

by inch into her tight pussy. When he was half way inside her, he pulled back out slightly and then pushed all the way to the hilt in one swift move.

Natalia gasped as she took all of him, worried he might have hurt her by going too fast, Taredd stayed motionless until she relaxed again underneath him. Only then did he begin to move again.

Taredd slid his cock in and out of her tight little pussy, slowly at first. It was heaven, so hot and wet, squeezing his cock perfectly. Releasing one of her legs, Taredd licked his thumb and then pressed it against the bundle of nerves just above where their bodies joined together.

Even with the large size of his cock, Natalia met him thrust for thrust as he fucked her harder and faster with each stroke. She didn't even complain when he grabbed both of her hips again and pounded into her so hard that the bed began to bang against the wall.

There was no way in hell that nobody in the building, or even walking past outside their room, didn't know what they were doing in here, and Taredd didn't give a shit either.

The entire world could walk in on them and see him fucking the life out of her for all he cared. They were more than welcome to take a seat and watch, but he wasn't going to stop for them.

The pleasure was so intense that he was finding it more difficult not to come. Especially when Natalia tipped over the edge as he pounded her. To stop himself from joining her, Taredd bit his lip so hard he tasted blood in his mouth.

Slowing down, he waited for the pulsing around his cock eased up before he finally stopped moving and pulled out of her completely.

Taredd wasn't going to give Natalia a chance to catch her breath. Flipping them both over so that Natalia was straddling his waist, he positioned her above his rock-hard cock.

Her eyes widen when she realized what he had in mind, but she didn't protest. Instead, she licked her lips and began to lower herself down. She moaned when his cock stretched her to her limits again.

Natalia arched her back when she was fully seated, thrusting her breasts out in front of her. Unable to resist the temptation, Taredd sat up and sucked one of her nipples into his mouth before she knew what was happening. Taredd was rewarded with a moan as she rubbed against his lap.

Grabbing the back of his head, Natalia held him to her breasts as he sucked on one and then the other, paying each one the same amount of attention with his mouth and hands. He massaged the breast and gently pulled the nipple that wasn't in his mouth at the time, so neither felt left out when his attention was on the other.

Natalia moaned as she gyrated on his lap, still holding his head tightly in place but unable to stay still any longer. Taredd nipped and licked the tip of each nipple before releasing them again. With one hand behind her head, Taredd pulled her face to his for a passionate kiss.

Releasing her head from his hand, he grabbed hold

of her hips and started to slowly lift her up and down on his cock. Taking the lead, Natalia broke the kiss and pushed him so he was lying back on the bed again. Placing her hands on his chest, she let his hands help her move until she found a rhythm of her own.

Soon, she was moving up and down on his cock without needing him to help. Her breasts bouncing along with her movements, tormenting him as they were just out of reach. Gliding his hands up the sides of her body so that he could cup her breasts. He used his fingers to massage her breasts and play with her nipples as she rode him as hard and fast as she could.

When her movements began to slow down, Taredd spun them around again. This time he placed her on all fours as he knelt behind her.

Before she had a chance to process this new position, he entered her in one swift move to the hilt. Natalia sucked in a breath at the sudden movement, so he paused for a moment so she could adjust to the new position.

Taredd was even deeper inside her in this position, so he needed to be patient as she adjusted to taking even more of him into her tight pussy. When she started rubbing and pushing up against him, he took the hint and began moving. Slowly at first so that he knew for sure she could take him this way, then he picked up the pace again.

Holding her in place, Taredd pounded into her so hard and fast that the bed slammed against the wall. He could feel her getting close to the edge again.

This time when she tipped over the edge, Taredd

followed her. Not that he had much choice in the matter, as her pussy squeezed his cock so tightly. Taredd roared out his release as Natalia screamed her orgasm into the bed.

When they were both finished, Taredd fell to his side on the bed, taking Natalia as he stayed buried deep inside her. With her back pressed up tight against his chest, Taredd could feel her heart pounding as she panted from exhaustion.

With one arm under her head, he cupped one of her breasts with his free hand and held her tightly against him as her breathing slowly returned to normal, and then finally evened out as she drifted back off to sleep.

Taredd didn't know how long he laid there like that, cock still buried inside her and cupping her breast, but when he finally managed to pull himself away from her, she was softly snoring.

Taredd didn't waste any time in cleaning himself and dressing. He needed some time and space away from Natalia to clear his head, even more so now after what they had just done.

Without looking back at the bed, Taredd left the room, locking the door behind him.

CHAPTER TWENTY-SEVEN

Natalia

As Natalia slowly woke up the next morning, she stretched across the bed and noticed straight away that Taredd was no longer in the bed with her. She would've thought that last night had all been a dream if her body didn't tell her otherwise.

Feeling a pang of hurt that Taredd wasn't still in bed with her, she tried not to let it bother her, but she failed. When Natalia sat up, she half expected him to be seated in the chair once again, smiling at her as if he hadn't moved an inch since she fell asleep, but he wasn't there either.

Fighting back the tears that threatened to spill, Natalia pulled the blankets up around herself. There was no way in hell she was going to let herself cry over a man, let alone a Demon, no matter how much he'd hurt her feelings.

Giving herself a mental slap, Natalia was about to climb out of bed when someone started banging on the door.

She shouted "One minute."

But before she had a chance to stand up and put

some clothes on, the door came crashing down as two Demons that looked similar to Taredd rushed into the room. Beelining it for her, Natalia didn't stand a chance against them as they viscously pulled her up out of bed and dragged her across the room, over the broken door and into the corridor.

"Help!" Natalia screamed at the top of her voice, but before any help could come to aid her, one of the Demons punched her hard in the face, knocking her out cold.

CHAPTER TWENTY-EIGHT

Taredd

Taredd used the time away from Natalia to try and clear his head, but it hadn't worked as he had planned. If anything, he was more confused than ever. It didn't matter how far, or how long, he walked in the crisp morning air, nothing helped change the way he felt about her.

After looking up at the sun, he'd realized he had been out walking for quite some time. Natalia had more than likely been awake for a while by the time he noticed, so he had turned around and headed back to the tavern, stopping along the way to grab some breakfast for them both.

Once he was back at the tavern, Taredd took the stairs two at a time. When he was in sight of their room, he stopped dead in his tracks. The door to their room was completely destroyed.

Snapping back into motion, Taredd raced straight into the room. He knew it was going to be empty before he even looked, but he needed to be certain.

"I thought that was you," Dain said from where he stood in the doorway.

Taredd spun on his heel and had Dain pinned up against the wall before he could take another breath.

"Where the fuck is she?" he growled.

With a confused look on his face, Dain held his arms up in surrender and asked "Where the fuck is who?"

"The female that was in this room. Where. Is. She?" he demanded.

"Dude, I don't know who the fuck you're talking about," Dain said, shaking his head. "I didn't even know you was here until I saw you walking into the tavern just a minute ago."

Letting go of Dain, Taredd backed away from him and started pacing the room.

"So, who is she?" Dain asked.

Instead of answering Dain's question, he asked one of his own "How long have you been here?"

"I've been in this town since you and Arun went off on your own," Dain said. "I didn't know you were here as well until I saw you heading in here, so I followed you to see how your hunt was going."

"I won the bet, if that's what you're asking," Taredd said.

"That's great, I knew you could do it!" Dain said excitedly.

"It's not great!" Taredd roared. "Because now she's missing!"

"So? Find another one," Dain told him as he shrugged his shoulders.

"I don't want another one," Taredd yelled as he hit the wall.

It was a choice of either the wall or Dain's face, and since Dain hadn't actually done anything wrong as far as Taredd knew, it was better he took his rage out on the wall instead.

"I can see that." Dain said, eyebrows raised as he looked at the hole Taredd had just made in the wall. "What's going on, Taredd? What makes this Human so special to you?"

"I made a promise to her that she wouldn't die."

"You what?"

Taredd could tell he had shocked Dain with his admission, but he didn't care anymore. All that matter now, was getting Natalia back.

He dreaded to think what could be happening to her while he stood around talking to Dain, but if he had any chance in getting her back safely, then he was going to need Dain's help.

"I promised that she wouldn't die," he repeated himself.

"Why the fuck would you promise a Human something like that?" Dain asked. "Have you forgotten what we do?"

"Of course, I haven't forgotten," Taredd said, shaking his head. "I don't know why I promised her, but I did, and now she's gone, so I've probably already broken my promise."

"There's more to it than just a promise, isn't there?" Dain asked him.

Taredd nodded. The problem was, he didn't know how to start explaining it to Dain. It still didn't make any sense to Taredd, so how the hell he expect Dain to understand it, when he didn't understand it himself?

Even still, Taredd filled Dain in as best as he could on everything that had happened since they split up. He admitted that he'd grown attached to Natalia, and did his best at explaining about the confusing feelings that were swirling around inside him.

Once Taredd was finally finished, Dain shook his head and said: "It sounds like you've fallen in love with this Human."

"That's not possible," Taredd said adamantly.

"Why's it not possible?" Dain asked. "You know as well as I do that anything is possible."

"Because, it's not," Taredd said. "I'm a Demon, for fuck sake. I hunt down and kill her kind, not fall in love with them."

"That doesn't mean it's not possible," Dain told him. "And from the looks of you, I would say that is exactly what's happened."

Taredd didn't want to agree with Dain, but he couldn't deny the evidence. It was the only explanation that made any sense of why he couldn't think straight around her. Why he acted the way he did when she was close to him, and why he was having this reaction now that she was gone.

No, not gone, taken. She was taken from him, but he swore to hell and high water that he was going to get her back. No matter what it took, she was going to be by his side once again.

"I need to find her, Dain," he said. "I can't lose her."

"You won't lose her, Taredd. I'll help you find her, no matter what it takes," Dain told him before he asked: "What do you need me to do?"

Taredd looked around the room. It didn't appear as if Natalia put up much of a fight, but even if there was only one assailant, she wouldn't have stood a chance against them.

It didn't matter what species it was, Natalia wouldn't have been able to fight against them, and he couldn't see it being one of her kind. They wouldn't have made it far into town on their own, let alone manage to drag Natalia out of here with them without being seen.

"I need your nose," he said out of the blue.

"Okay," Dain said, dragging out the word. "What do you need my nose for?"

"Why the fuck do you think?" Taredd said, rolling his eyes. "I want you to follow her scent."

"Ah, I see. You want me to be your personal sniffer dog," Dain said dryly.

"Something like that," Taredd admitted, shrugging a shoulder. "So, come on then, shift already."

"Fine," Dain gave in. "I'll do it, but you tell Arun I did this for you and I'll flat out deny it."

"I promise not to say a thing to Arun about this," Taredd swore. "Just hurry up and shift already."

"Okay, okay," Dain said.

A moment later, he was stood on four paws. Taredd thought Dain would have chosen to shift into a wolf like he normally would have done, but instead this time he shifted into a bloodhound.

"Really?" Taredd asked him with an eyebrow raised.

When Dain growled at him, Taredd couldn't help but laugh at him.

"I already said I wouldn't tell Arun," he said, holding his hands up. "I didn't agree not to laugh though."

When Dain growled again, Taredd added: "Fine, I won't laugh either. Just get on with sniffing around already."

Dain growled once more before getting on with the task at hand. When he picked up her scent, he barked at Taredd and raced out the room. Taredd kept up easily with Dain as he tracked down Natalia, neither of them slowed until they came to a rundown building a few blocks away from the tavern.

Taredd recognized the building, he remembered walking past here after he left Natalia sleeping this morning. They must have seen him with her the day before and assumed he had left her alone in the tavern... which he had done... and taken the opportunity to snatch her from him.

It didn't matter who they were, they wouldn't have stood a chance against him if he had been there, which is probably why they waited until they had seen him on his own without her.

Dain shifted back into himself when they were outside the building. "She's in there."

Looking up at the building, Taredd asked: "Do you know how many people are in there with her?"

"I can't say for sure without going in there and taking a closer look," Dain told him. "But there were two different scents in the room with her, so it's more than likely that at least two people took her from your room."

"We can't go in there without knowing what we'll be walking into," Taredd said. "For all we know, it could put her in even greater danger than she already is."

"True," Dain agreed.

"I need to do something though, anything could be happening to her."

"I know," Dain told him.

They were both silent for a moment, trying to think of the best course of action.

Dain was the one to break the silence, when he said: "Wait out of sight of the building, I'll go in and check the place out, see what we're up against. It's not a massive building, so it shouldn't take me long."

"Okay," he said, forcing himself to back away. "But, hurry up."

"I will," Dain said right before he shifted into a mouse.

Once Dain had vanished into the building, Taredd moved closer again. He couldn't just stand around doing nothing. He didn't lie to Dain when he said he couldn't go in there until he knew what he was up against, but there was nothing to stop him from looking through the windows and seeing for himself.

As long as he was careful and stayed out of sight, Taredd should be able to sneak around the outside unnoticed. Peeking through the windows turned out to be a complete waste of time though, he couldn't see a damn thing through the dirt and muck covering them.

Fuck! This was not how he had envisioned today going, not one bit.

Moving back away from the building, he had no

other choice but to wait for Dain to come back with some usable intel. Even without knowing what he was up against, Taredd knew without a doubt it would be a hell of a lot easier if Arun was here as well.

If it wasn't for this fucking stupid bet, then he would have been, but then he might not have got so close to Natalia either. He would have just killed her straight away and wouldn't have gotten to know the strong, sassy, and sexy female that she was.

He wouldn't have had the honour of pleasuring her body either, which would be a crying shame in its self. She had been so responsive to his every touch, even going so far as to beg for more. And he wanted to give her more. He already craved the taste of her... he craved all of her.

Taredd swore when she was safely back with him, he was never again going to leave her side.

CHAPTER TWENTY-NINE

Natalia

Natalia woke from the pounding in her face and head. It took only seconds for everything to come flooding back to her. Looking around at her new surroundings she knew for sure that she was no longer in the tavern.

She didn't have a clue where she was, but there was no doubt in her mind that she wasn't in the same building she'd been in with Taredd. Whoever grabbed her had taken her somewhere else.

"Where the fuck am I?" she shouted out to anyone that could hear her.

Not expecting a reply, Natalia nearly jumped out of her skin when a deep male voice said: "You're in my home."

Her head instantly snapped in the direction the voice came from, and there stood a group of Demons. The two who snatched her from the tavern were there, as well as another three she hadn't seen before.

All of them had a similar appearance to each other, but other than having the same skin colour, none of them looked anything like Taredd.

From the looks on the faces of these Demons, there was no way in hell they were going to promise not to kill her like Taredd had done. In fact, it looked as if they couldn't wait to tear her apart. They were more of the type that would take great pleasure in causing her as much pain as possible.

"What do you want with me?" she asked them.

"What do you think we want with you?" The same person as last time answered her, so she could see which one she was dealing with.

"I don't know," she said, playing dumb.

"You can play coy with me as much as you like," he told her. "But you already know the answer to that question."

"Maybe," she admitted. "But just so we're all on the same page, tell me anyway."

Natalia could see this Demon wasn't going to find her as entertaining as Taredd seemed to have, it would help if she knew how she entertained Taredd to begin with, then she might have tried doing the same with these Demons... not that it looked as if it would work on them though.

If anything, she was more than likely going to make them want to cause her even more pain before finishing her off. The Demon in charge however, still played along, still answered her.

"We're going to have some fun with you," he told her.

"I like fun," she said.

With a sinister laugh, he said: "I didn't say it was going to be fun for you."

The other Demons standing next to him all started laughing as well. A sick feeling entered Natalia's stomach, and she had to fight down the bile that was creeping up her throat.

She wished Taredd was here with her. Natalia knew he would keep her safe if he was. She didn't know how she knew he would, she just did.

"It seems a bit unfair, and doesn't seem like much fun if I don't fight back," she told them, trying to trick them into releasing her so she could try to escape, or at least, stall them as much as she could.

Natalia didn't know if it would work, but she was trying to stall for time in the hopes that Taredd was going to rescue her. She knew it was unlikely that he was going to burst through those doors and save her, but she couldn't stop the small sliver of hope that he might.

It was possible he didn't even knew she was missing, let alone be on his way here now to rescue her, but it still didn't stop her.

The demon in charge thought about her comment for a moment. She could see the wheels turning in his head as he thought about how much more fun it would be for him if she fought against him.

When he came to a decision, he turned to the others with him and demanded "Leave us."

"But..." One of the others was about to complain, but stopped when the one in charged pouched him square in the face, knocking him out cold.

"Anyone else have something to say?" he asked the others, all of which shook their heads. "Good. Now, take him and leave."

Without another word, they left the room, taking their fallen comrade with them and shutting the door behind themselves.

"Now that we're alone," he said with an evil grin on his face as he walked towards her. "Shall we begin?"

Natalia swallowed hard. Now she was definitely in trouble.

CHAPTER THIRTY

Taredd

Taredd didn't know what was taking Dain so long to scout the building. Yes, he was the size of a mouse, but it was only a three-story building with no more than half a dozen rooms on each floor.

Taredd was about to go in after Dain, when suddenly a mouse appeared in front of him and then transformed into the Dain he was used to seeing.

"It's not good," Dain said without preamble as Taredd rushed over to him. "There's a dozen Demons in there, one of which has just shut himself in a room with who I'm assuming is your Human female."

That was it, Taredd couldn't wait any longer. Storming straight over to the building with Dain hot on his heels, he didn't bother to knock on the door when he reached it. Instead, he lifted his foot and kicked it in like they had with the bedroom door back at the tavern.

"Where is she?" he demanded from Dain as shouting erupted from everywhere in the building.

"Third floor, last room on the left," Dain quickly replied.

Taredd didn't hang around downstairs waiting for the Demons to come to him. He headed straight up the stairs, swiftly ending the lives of anyone that stepped in his way. Between himself and Dain, they ripped apart every Demon that came at them, throwing their lifeless bodies down the stairs behind them.

When they reach the room where she was being held, Dain split off so he could hunt down any other Demons that were lurking around the building, while Taredd went in to rescue Natalia.

Without hesitation, Taredd kicked the door down and burst into the room just in time to see a male Demon pinning Natalia face down on a bed. The Demon was posed above her, about to rape her.

Seeing red at the sight of Natalia laying underneath the Demon with tears gleaming in her eyes, Taredd stormed over to the bed and grabbed the Demon by the back of the neck. Taredd then threw the Demon as hard as he could against the wall on the opposite side of the room.

Before the Demon had a chance to recover, Taredd was on him once again. This time, instead of throwing him again, Taredd pinned him against the wall and grabbing the males dick, ripping it straight off his body without any effort.

When the Demon opened his mouth in a silent scream, Taredd stuffed the severed dick into his mouth.

Still not satisfied, Taredd began pummelling the Demons face with his fist until he was unrecognizable. Then he ripped the male's body in half, and throwing it to either side of himself.

Covered in blood, Taredd turned around to face Natalia. She was sat in a ball, cuddling her legs against herself as her body shook. Taredd slowly walked over to the bed again. He crouched down in front of her and reached out his arms.

Natalia didn't hesitate, even seeing that he was covered in blood from the many Demons he killed trying to reach her, she threw herself into his open arms and clung tightly to him.

"I'm sorry," he whispered into her ear as he held her tightly, stroking the back of her hair. "I'm so sorry."

Natalia didn't say a word as silent tears fell from her eyes as she held on to him.

"Is she okay?" Dain asked as he walked in the room.

"She will be," Taredd told him.

She was going to be okay because Taredd was going to make sure she was, even if it was the last thing he ever did.

Looking over his shoulder at Dain, he said: "Her clothes are shredded to pieces, can you find something to cover her with so we can get out of here?"

"Yeah, of course. I think I saw a blanket in one of the other rooms," Dain said as he turned and hurried to grab one of the blankets for her.

"Natalia, look at me," he coaxed. When she did, he told her "You're safe now, my love."

"I knew you would come for me," she whispered.

"Always," he told her. "I will always come for you."

Dain came rushing back in the room a moment later, carrying a large blanket in his hands. It wasn't the cleanest blanket in the world, but it would do to get her back to the tavern without anyone seeing her naked body, because the bits of fabric still hanging on her barely covered anything.

"Here you go." Dain handed it to Taredd. "This should be big enough."

"Thanks," he said, taking it from Dain so he could wrap it around Natalia.

She didn't say a word, but she did look warily at Dain.

"Don't worry about him," Taredd told her. "This is Dain, one of the friends I was telling you about."

"Hi," she said quietly.

"It's nice to meet you." Dain bowed his head. "But I'm sorry it had to be under these circumstances."

Not giving Natalia a chance to protest, as soon as she was completely wrapped up in the blanket, Taredd slid his arms underneath her and gently picked her up, then stood and carried her out of the room.

It didn't matter if she could walk easily enough on her own, Taredd wanted… needed… to hold her tight against him. If that meant carrying her all the way back to the tavern with her protesting the entire way, then so be it.

CHAPTER THIRTY-ONE

Natalia

While Natalia was grateful Taredd had reached her before she was raped, he hadn't managed to rescue her in time to prevent the beating she'd taken. Her whole body hurt from where he used her as his personal punching bag before ripping her clothes to shreds.

Natalia didn't complain about Taredd carrying her back to the tavern. She could have walked back easily enough on her own, but Taredd refused to put her down.

She didn't have the strength to argue with him. So, instead of insisting that he put her down, she held on tightly as he carried her effortlessly back to the tavern.

Taredd's friend didn't say much as they walk along either, which suited her just find because she was in no mood for small talk. Natalia didn't have a clue what species Dain was, but she could tell that he wasn't a Demon like Taredd.

For starters, he didn't have any horns on the top of his head. Well, at least none that she could see anyway.

The blanket Dain found for her didn't help her body

feel any better. It rubbed against the cuts that were all over her skin, but she was grateful all the same. After all, it covered her body since her clothing couldn't do the job after being ripped to shreds.

The small amount of fabric remaining from her clothing was barely holding together, and it definitely wasn't enough to cover her.

By the time they reached the tavern, Natalia found it hard to fight back the tears. She wanted to lock herself away so nobody could see her cry, least of all Taredd. Not once did his hold on her loosen at any point on the walk back. The way he held her so tightly made her think that he was afraid of letting go and dropping her.

Natalia didn't want him to think of her as weak, which was one of the reasons she was fighting so hard not to cry in front of him and his friend. She knew that being carried by him would make her appear that way, but she didn't have a choice in the matter. That didn't mean she was going to burst into tears in front of him though.

"We're here now," he whispered in her ear as he climbed the stairs two at a time with her still in his arms.

Natalia nudged him with her head to let him know that she heard him. She didn't trust her voice not to give away how close she was to tears.

Once they were in the room, Taredd lowered her to her feet and Natalia instantly excused herself.

"I'm gonna take a bath," she said quietly.

With her head lowered, holding on tight to the blanket so she didn't drop it, she made her way to the bathroom without saying another word.

"Okay," Taredd replied. "Just shout for me if you need anything, I'll be in here."

Natalia nodded her head, but didn't look back as she closed the door behind her.

As soon as the water was running, Natalia let loose the tears that had been threatening to fall since the moment Taredd had found her. They soaked her cheeks in seconds even though she kept wiping them away, and no matter how hard she tried, now that the floodgates were open, she couldn't close them again.

Natalia didn't wait for the bath to fill completely. Climbing into the bath when it was half filled, Natalia bit her bottom lip as the water stung her cuts. Closing her eyes, she laid back in the water to wet her hair, but when she didn't stop crying, she sat up again.

Holding her legs to her chest, she let the tears fall unchecked. There was no point in fighting them, so she might as well let them have free reign.

It seemed to take forever before they finally stopped, she was completely exhausted by the time they did. Natalia didn't have the energy to move, let alone wash herself. So, she just sat there as the water started to go cold around her, waiting for her energy to return for her to move, at least enough for her to add some hot water so she could finish bathing.

CHAPTER THIRTY-TWO

Taredd

Taredd was fuming. It was all his fault that those Demons managed to get their hands on Natalia. If he hadn't left her alone in the tavern, then none of this would have happened.

If he hadn't forced her to go with him in the first place, then none of this would have happened because she wouldn't have been in a town full of monsters as she called them.

Because of his ignorance in thinking she was safe after being seen with him, she had been hurt and there was nothing he could do to change it, he couldn't turn back time and change the past. Now he would have to live with himself for causing her harm, it didn't matter what anyone said, it was all his fault.

At least she didn't have to come back here to see the destruction left in the Demons wake. While they had been gone, the broken door had been replaced with a new one. Taredd was impressed at how quickly they had cleaned up the mess.

"Stop blaming yourself," Dain told him. "You couldn't have known any of this would happen."

"I should have known though," he said, pacing the room.

Natalia was in the other room still, soaking in the bath. He could hear her crying as she sat in the rapidly cooling water. Taredd would do anything he could to take away her pain, but there wasn't anything that he could do.

"Why should you have known?" Dain asked.

"Because I knew that we were being watched. I should have known it was only a matter of time before they were going to do something," he said, adamantly. "I should have never left her alone."

"Taredd…"

"It doesn't matter what you say, Dain," he interrupted. "It will not change a thing. It was my fault, and there's nothing you can say that will change my mind."

Stopping in front of the door separating him from Natalia, he put his hand against it and said quietly. "I just hope she can forgive me."

Dain walked over and placed his hand on Taredd shoulder, but he didn't say a thing. Dain knew he was right, so there wasn't much he could say.

Moving away from the door, Taredd began pacing again. He couldn't sit still while she was in there, hurting. He wanted to comfort her, but he didn't know how. The cuts and bruises would heal in time, but the memory of what happened to her would take longer to fade, if it ever did.

"I'm taking her home," he said suddenly.

"What?" Dain asked.

"I'm taking her home," he repeated, turning to look Dain in the eyes.

"You know where she lives?" Dain asked with a raised eyebrow.

"I do now," he said confidently.

"Don't tell me that you're going to do what I think you are?" Dain asked, shaking his head.

"I'm taking her back to my home."

"But your home is in the Demon realm," Dain pointed out. "If you're trying to keep her safe, do you think that is the best place to take her?"

"There's no place safer than my home," Taredd told him.

Even being in the Demon realm she was far safer than staying in this realm. There were more than enough people working for him back home to keep her safe. He trusted every single one of them not to cause Natalia any harm.

If they knew what she meant to him, then they would lay down their lives to protect her from other Demons living in the realm. So, yes, it was the safest place to take her.

Now he just needed to convince her it was the best thing for her. That might not be so easy, especially after what had just happened to her.

"Okay," Dain said. "But you're going to need both mine and Arun's help in getting her to your house in one piece. You know it's more dangerous for Humans in the Demon realm than it is here."

Taredd turned and looked at Dain. "You don't have to do that," he told him.

"Yes, I do." Dain nodded his head. "You would do the same for us if it was the other way around."

"How do you know I wouldn't just kill the Human you had fallen for?" Taredd asked him.

"Because you're not like that," he said adamantly. "Neither am I or Arun, and you know it, especially not after the way I've seen you with her."

"Okay," Taredd agreed. "You can help."

"Why, thank you," Dain said with a smile. "But just so you know, I wasn't actually giving you a choice in the matter."

Taredd shook his head as he smiled. He should have known Dain wouldn't let him do this alone.

"Now, we need to find Arun," Dain told him. "I know for a fact he wouldn't want to miss the action that's bound to be ahead of us."

"Fine, but if he so much as looks at Natalia the wrong way, I will kill him," Taredd told him.

"Arun will not touch a hair on Natalia's pretty little head," Dain told him.

"How do you know that? He doesn't know what's going on or how I feel about her," Taredd said. "He could attack her before he finds out."

"That's not like Arun, and you know it," Dain pointed out again.

Deep down Taredd did know Arun wasn't like that, but it still didn't stop the worry floating around in his head where Natalia was concerned.

"Yeah, I know," he admitted. "It's just..."

"I know, your head is up your ass where she's concerned," Dain interrupted.

"Yeah, something like that," Taredd admitted.

"Dude, you don't have to tell me, I know how much females can affect your way of thinking," Dain told him.

If anyone really did understand how Taredd was feeling, it would be Dain. His kind were extremely possessive when it came to their females, especially when their female's life was in danger.

"So, what's the plan?" Dain asked after a moments silence.

"I don't know yet."

"Well, the first thing I think we need to do, is find Arun," Dain told him.

"That could take days," Taredd said. "Unless you know where he went?"

"Nah, I only know which direction he was heading in."

"At least that's a start." Taredd looked at the closed bathroom door. "But we can't go anywhere until Natalia is up to it."

"I can't see that being today, so, I'll go see if there's another room available for the night," Dain said as he headed towards the door.

"Good idea."

"Yeah, I know, I'm full of good ideas," Dain said jokingly.

Taredd couldn't help but smile as he shook his head.

"I'll be back in a couple of minutes," he said just before closing the door behind himself.

Taredd continued to pace the room. He wanted to let himself in to the bathroom and comfort Natalia, or at least have her come out so he could hold her close. How the hell she had come to mean so much to him in such a short period of time, he didn't know, and he didn't care either. All he cared about now, was Natalia.

Walking back over to the bathroom door, he gently tapped on it. When she didn't reply, he said: "Natalia, are you okay in there?"

He knew it was a stupid question, he could hear that she wasn't okay. Even knowing that, he still couldn't help asking her.

"I'll be okay." Came her weak reply.

Not believing her for one second, he asked: "Can I come in?"

It took her a moment before she said: "Yes."

Taredd could have kicked himself when he realized the door wasn't locked the whole time he had been pacing outside. He could have just let himself in at any moment, instead of being stuck out here worrying about her.

Pushing the door open, he entered the room and shut the door again behind him. Natalia was seated in the bath with her knees pulled up to her chest. Taredd walked over and knelt down next to her.

"Are you okay?" he asked, brushing a wet strand of hair off her face.

Even if he hadn't heard her through the door, he would have known she had been crying, he could see it, just by the look in her eyes.

"I'll be okay," she lied to him, and he let her.

Stoking her hair, he said: "I'm going to take you back home when you're ready. You'll be safe there, I promise."

Natalia didn't say anything, she just nodded her head in agreement.

"I'm sorry I wasn't here to protect you."

"It wasn't your fault," she told him without hesitation.

"It was," he told her. "But I promise it will never happen again."

"You can't promise that," she told him.

"Yes, I can. Because I'm never letting you out of my sight again. I will never leave you alone ever again," he assured her.

Taredd didn't know if it was wishful thinking or not, but he could have sworn he saw a spark of hope in her eyes for a second before it disappeared again.

"Natalia, look at me," he said, gently lifting her chin so she faced him.

It took her a moment, but when she finally looked into his eyes, he told her: "I'm never going to let you out of my sight again."

"But..."

"But what?"

"You said you're taking me home, but you already told me you don't like the bunkers, so how can you keep an eye on me if I'm in there?"

"Because..." he said as he leaned in and kissed her on the tip of her nose. "... we're going to my home."

"Oh," she said, surprised by his answer.

"I can keep you safe there," he promised her.

Natalia closed her eyes and took a deep breath.

"Okay," she said. "When are we leaving?"

"Not today," he told her. "You need to rest today. We will leave tomorrow if you're ready, because it's going to be a long journey."

He decided to keep it to himself that it was more than likely going to be an extremely dangerous journey, but if everything went as planned, then they should all make it there in one piece. And Dain was right, for that to happen he needed both him and Arun by his side.

CHAPTER THIRTY-THREE

Natalia

Later that day, Natalia decided after all Taredd had done for her that he deserved the truth. Since the moment they first met, he has done nothing but be open and honest about everything, even when he didn't have to be.

He hadn't bothered to hide the fact that he hunted down and killed her kind. He hadn't even hidden the fact he had a bet going with his friend, which is why he hadn't just killed her right in the beginning.

Not only that, but Taredd has gone out of his way time and again to make sure she was well fed. He even went out of his way to find her a proper bed for the night. He could have just made her sleep rough again, but he didn't. So, the least she could do was be as open and honest with him in return.

Natalia just needed to make sure that he would treat her friends the same way he had been treating her. Even if he just promised not to kill them it would be a good start. He didn't need to treat them exactly the same, as long as they were as safe around him and his friends as she was, she would be happy.

In fact, the thought of him getting as close to any of the women in her group... Amberly included... made her want to keep him away from any of them. She trusted Amberly with her life, but she still didn't want to share Taredd with her.

Natalia didn't know how... or when... she became so possessive over Taredd, but she had. She wasn't going to deny her feelings towards him any longer, especially from herself. There was no way she was going to admit it out loud, or let Taredd know her feelings just yet, but she couldn't deny it to herself anymore.

As soon as they were alone again after Dain had brought them something to eat, Natalia finally plucked up the courage to tell Taredd about her friends.

Hoping for the best, she blurted it out. "I can't leave this area without finding my friends first."

Looking over at her, his brows pinched together. "What?" he asked, confused.

"I want to go with you to your home, but I can't leave my friends behind," she told him.

"How many friends are we talking about?" he asked.

Natalia was surprised by his question, she hadn't expected him to ask how many. She had expected him to just say 'no chance'. But as usual, he was still surprising her by doing the unexpected.

"I... I don't know," she told him honestly.

Natalia couldn't be sure how many were left in the group since she split up from them. It had been a long time, and they had travelled a long way, anything could have happened to her group. She just hoped

Amberly and Donovan were still together and safe.

"Okay, how many was there when you were last with them?"

"Eight."

"Eight?" he asked, raising his brows.

"Yes."

Taredd took a deep breath. "Do you know where they are?"

"No," she admitted.

"That's going to make things a little harder," he told her before asking "Do you at least know which area they might be in?"

"No," she said, looking down at her hands in her lap. "I'm sorry I can't be more helpful, but they could be anywhere by now. None of us know this area very well, so we didn't have a plan of where to meet up again."

"Don't worry about it, we'll figure something out," he said, walking over to sit next to her on the bed.

"Thank you," she said as he pulled her against him.

"Where was it you last saw them?" he asked.

"It was on the other side of the mountain pass," she told him. "We were supposed to meet up somewhere when I got here, but then I bumped into you so I haven't been able to look for them."

"Why didn't you travel with them through the mountains?"

"Because of Bella," Natalia said, rolling her eyes. "She's this really annoying girl who was in our group. She wondered off when we were at the beginning of the pass. We didn't notice that she had wondered off straight away, but when we did, we decided that someone needed to go back and make sure she was okay and nothing bad had happened to her."

"And that someone had to be you?" he asked.

"Well, yes, I was the leader of our group, so it was my responsibility to make sure she was okay."

"Why didn't you take anyone with you?"

"Because it was safer if they went ahead." In hindsight, she probably should have, but after everything that had happened to her since separating from them, she was glad she hadn't taken anyone with her.

"Safer for them, maybe," he told her.

Natalia had the feeling he was pissed off, but she didn't know why.

"Yes, it was safer for them," Natalia said, looking up at him. "It was my job to keep them safe."

"Not anymore it isn't," he said sternly.

"Of course, it is."

"No, now it's my job. Like it's my job to keep you safe."

Natalia didn't know what to say. She was hoping he would promise not to kill her friends, but she never expected him to take on the responsibility of keeping them safe as well.

"So," he said. "We'll tell Dain tomorrow that we need to find them as well as Arun."

"Thank you," she finally said.

"You're welcome."

Natalia couldn't stop the tears from falling in front of him this time. Instead of pushing her away, or saying something about them, Taredd pulled her closer into his arms and held her tightly while she quietly sobbed.

Even though she tried not to show it, she had been so frightened to tell him about her friends, and even more frightened when the other Demons had hold of her. Especially when she was alone with one of them. It wasn't so much the beating he gave her, it was more the fact that if Taredd hadn't arrived when he did, that monster would have raped her.

Natalia knew she was lucky Taredd turned up in time. She didn't know how she was going to repay him for rescuing her, but she owed him her life, if not more.

When she eventually stopped crying again, Natalia couldn't keep her eyes open any longer, so she didn't bother fighting it. Feeling like a child safe in Taredd's arms, she drifted off to sleep.

CHAPTER THIRTY-FOUR

Taredd

Taredd didn't want to let Natalia go, ever. Even when she was fast asleep in his arms, completely worn out from crying, he held on to her tightly.

Only when there was a light tapping on the bedroom door did he finally move out from under her. Gently rolling her onto her side, he pulled the covers up around her and tucked her in.

He quietly made his way over to the door and opened it to see Dain standing on the other side, with a tray full of food in his hands.

Holding his finger up to his lips, Taredd whispered: "Shush, she's finally asleep."

"I thought you could both do with some more food to eat," Dain whispered back.

"Thank you," Taredd said, opening the door wider for Dain to enter. "Come in, but be quiet because I don't want Natalia to wake up, she needs to rest as much as she can."

"I promise not to wake her, especially not on purpose," Dain said as he carried the tray in and placed it quietly on the table.

"Cheers for bring some more food, I'm starving," Taredd said as he sat in the chair from the night before.

Between Natalia's crying, and then her sleeping in his arms, hours had passed since they had last eaten..

"You're welcome," Dain said, as he sat on the only other chair in the room. "I didn't think you would want to leave her to get it yourself."

"And you were right," Taredd told him.

Dain waited until Taredd had eaten some of the food, before asking anything about the plans to find Arun. But now Taredd had to fill him in on Natalia's friends as well, making both their lives more complicated, but he didn't care.

He would do anything to make Natalia happy, and finding her friends would definitely make her happy.

"So, what's the plan for tomorrow?" Dain eventually asked.

"We need to track down Arun, and then find Natalia's friends," he said, looking at her sleeping form in the bed.

"Her friends?" Dain asked.

"Yeah, apparently there's eight of them."

"Shit," Dain said. "What are we going to do with that many of them?"

"To be honest with you, I don't have a fucking clue," he said, shaking his head. "But she says she can't leave without them, so we've got to find them."

"I take it that she doesn't know where they are either?" Dain asked.

"That's correct."

"Wonderful. Nothing like a mass man hunt to start the day," Dain said.

"Don't bitch, I know you enjoy it," Taredd told him. "It's not much different than being on a hunt."

"Yeah, it is," Dain said. "I get to kill my prey once I've found it when we're on a hunt."

"Well, you can't kill these ones," Taredd said sternly.

"I know that. I'm not stupid," Dain said, shaking his head. "That would just upset Natalia, and I know you would kill me if I did something like that."

"Yes, I would," Taredd agreed. "And, I would take great pleasure in doing so."

"Don't lie," Dain told him. "You and Arun would be lost without me."

"I don't think we would," Taredd told him. "But... it wouldn't be as much fun without you."

"See? I knew you cared," Dain said smugly.

"I wouldn't go that far," Taredd said. "But yeah, it wouldn't be the same without you... or Arun."

"Yeah, the grumpy old git grows on you, doesn't he."?

"I wonder if he's caught a Human of his own yet?" Taredd asked.

"Probably not, knowing him," Dain said. "It wouldn't surprise me if he was still looking for one, let alone actually caught one."

"Yeah, that's true." Taredd laughed quietly. "He's not the best at tracking, is he."

"Nope," Dain agreed. "I think that's why he hangs around with us."

"He's probably wondering around like a headless chicken without us there helping him," Dain said, laughing as well, just not as quietly as Taredd had done.

Dain instantly stopped when Natalia groaned as she turned over in her sleep. If they weren't quieter, then they were going to wake her up. It wouldn't be such a bad thing, because she needed to eat as well, but he wanted her to get a little bit more rest before she woke.

The food would still be okay if she slept longer, so there was no rush to eat it before it turned bad.

"Anyway," Dain said as he stood and stretched before heading to the door. "I'm gonna leave you two in peace."

"Okay, we'll see you in the morning."

"If you need anything, I'll be right next door," he said, pointing in the direction of his room.

"We should be fine for tonight," Taredd told him.

"Well, the offers there if you change your mind."

"Dain?" Taredd said as he was about to shut the door. When Dain looked back at him, Taredd said: "Thanks for today."

"Any time," Dain said, smiling.

As tempting as it was to climb in bed next to Natalia again tonight, Taredd didn't want to disturb her. So instead, he kept watch over her from the chair.

CHAPTER THIRTY-FIVE

Natalia

Natalia had been hoping that Taredd would have joined her in the bed again last night while she was sleeping, but he hadn't. Instead, he had just stayed in the chair all night. She wasn't sure if he slept at all, but she had a feeling the answer to that was going to be no.

As soon as she had opened her eyes, she noticed that he was watching her.

"How long have I been asleep?" she asked.

"All afternoon and on into the night."

"Shit, I'm sorry, I didn't mean to sleep that long," she said, shaking her head. "You should have woken me."

"No, I shouldn't have, you needed the rest," he told her before he asked: "Are you hungry?"

Natalia didn't need to reply, her stomach did that for her as it rumbled loudly, but she still said: "Yes, I'm starving."

"Dain dropped off some fresh food this morning," he told her, pointing to the table next to him.

Natalia sat up in the bed and looked at the array of

different food for her to choose from.

"Have you eaten?" she asked him.

"Yes, I've had plenty," he told her. "This is all for you."

"I can't eat all of that," Natalia said looking at how much food was there.

"You don't have to eat it all," Taredd said, smiling. "Just eat what you want, I'm sure Dain will finish the rest."

Natalia couldn't help but smile in return. Every time Taredd smiled at her, it sent butterflies off in her stomach. Natalia still couldn't quite believe that she'd had sex with him, she didn't regret giving herself to him though.

That must be worthy of going in the history books. A Human having a sexual relationship with a Demon... willingly... was quite possibly a first all around. Well, it was definitely a drastic change from them killing her kind.

Natalia wondered what Amberly would say to her about it. She hoped her friend wouldn't disown her for it. Natalia didn't want to choose between Taredd and her friends.

Climbing out of bed, Natalia realized she was naked and quickly covered herself with the blanket off the bed.

"Sorry," she said, blushing.

With a sexy grin, Taredd said: "No need to be sorry, I enjoy seeing your body."

Blushing even more, Natalia asked: "Did you strip me?" Indicating with a wave of her hand to her lack of clothing.

Natalia didn't think it was him, but she still asked anyway, just in case he did have a hand in it.

"Nope, that was all you," he said, grinning from ear to ear. "Just like the night before."

Only this time she didn't have on her knickers and vest top underneath. Nope, after her bath Natalia had slipped on a pair of shorts and a t-shit, thinking that she would be safe from stripping since she didn't have many clothes on to begin with. That'll teach her to try to trick her unconscious mind.

"Yeah, I thought so," she said. "Sorry about that."

"Just so that I know, is it something you do on a regular basis?" he asked. "It's just, you didn't do it the first night when we slept under the stars, so I'm wondering if that night was a fluke."

"Yeah, it happens a lot," she told him. "But strangely enough, it only happens when I'm sleeping in a bed."

It had always confused her as to why it only happened to her when she was asleep in an actual bed, but she was glad it didn't happen any other time. It could have been a real problem if she had done something like that when she was sleeping in the caves along the mountain pass, or anywhere else just as dangerous.

"Good to know," Taredd told her. "I wouldn't want to kill one of my best friends just because he accidentally saw you strip naked in the middle of the night while we're between stops."

"Urm... yeah... I wouldn't want that to happen

either," she said, unsure if he meant it or not.

Natalia wouldn't want him to kill anyone for her... well, except for the Demons that had kidnapped her, she was glad he had killed them. But she certainly wouldn't want him to kill his friends because of something none of them could control or prevent.

"Dain isn't a Demon, is he?" she asked.

"No, he's a Shapeshifter," Taredd told her.

"Is your other friend a Shapeshifter, or a Demon?"

"Neither," he smiled. "Arun's a Fae.

Wrapping the blanket tighter around herself, she shuffled over to the empty chair next to Taredd. As soon as she was settled, he slid the table closer for her.

"Thank you," she said.

"You're welcome."

Natalia didn't know where to start, there was so much food to choose from that she ended up sitting there staring at it all for a couple of minutes before finally diving in.

"None of it's poisonous, if that's what you're worried about," Taredd told her.

"I know," she said. "I trust you."

"What's the problem then?"

"There's just so much to choose from. I've never had such a wide variety to choose from before," she told him honestly.

Most of the time Natalia was lucky to have breakfast. It wasn't as much of a priority as lunch or dinner, so more often than not, everyone skipped it. All except for any children in the group, but there hadn't been any children in their group for many years.

"Here," Taredd said, passing her a plate with some flat looking bread on it. "Try this. I think you'll like it."

Taking the plate from him, she held it up to her face and sniffed. Luckily enough it didn't smell like the fish. Natalia didn't think she could stomach anything that smelt that bad at this time of the morning. Dinner maybe, but definitely not for breakfast.

"Mmm..." Natalia moaned after she finally took a bit.

She didn't know if it was because she was hungry, or if the food really did taste this good, but it was the best she had ever eaten before. Light and fluffy like freshly baked bread, but with a sweet taste.

"Next time you see Dain, please tell him I said thank you," she told Taredd.

"You can tell him yourself," Taredd said. "He should be back soon."

"Where's he gone?" she asked, unsure if Taredd would actually tell her.

But Taredd didn't hesitate in telling her. "He's sorting out some transport for us."

"Transport?" she asked, confused.

"Yeah, just a horse and cart."

"Really?" she asked excitedly.

"Yes, really," he told her.

Natalia knew people used to use different modes of transport before the great war, but since then Humans had moved from place to place by foot. Motor vehicles didn't work anymore, she didn't know what caused them to stop working, but as soon as the war started anything motorized or mechanical all of a sudden stopped working.

Animals were another form of transport her kind used as well, but when some of the beings that were hunting them could turn into one of them, then it made it more difficult to know which was a real animal and which was a monster in disguise. So, they were left with using their own two feet to get them from point A to point B.

"Wow, I've never been on a horse and cart before," she told him. "We always travel by foot. Have you been on one before?"

"A few times over the years, but mostly on horseback.," he told her. "This time however, we'll be sitting on the cart as the horses pull us."

"That sounds fun," she said excitedly.

"Well, when Dain is back, and as soon as you're ready, we can leave," he told her.

Bouncing with excitement, Natalia jumped up,nearly losing her grip on the blanket in the process, and threw herself into Taredd arms. Wrapping her arms around his neck, she kissed him square on the lips before bounding over to the bathroom.

"I'll have a really quick bath," she said, then stopped suddenly to turn and face him. "Is that okay? Is there enough time?"

Nodding with a smile on his face, Taredd said: "Yes, there's more than enough time. Take as long as you want."

"Thank you," she said as she spun on her heels and all but ran into the bathroom.

Shutting the door behind her, she didn't waste any time in running the bath. As soon as it had a couple of inches of water in it, she jumped in. Unlike the night before, Natalia didn't sit around crying, she swiftly washed before climbing out again.

Just as she was drying herself, she heard a knock at the bedroom door. She listened as Taredd spoke with Dain about the travel arrangements. She heard him say that it could take them a good couple of days before they could find their friend Arun.

Just before the door closed, Taredd told Dain that she was having a quick bath and that they shouldn't be too long, so to wait for them downstairs. Natalia couldn't help thinking that this was probably going to be the last time they were going to be alone together for some time, so she wanted to make the most of the time they had left.

Taking a deep breath for courage, Natalia dropped the towel and opened the bathroom door before she could change her mind.

CHAPTER THIRTY-SIX

Taredd

The last thing that Taredd had expected, was for Natalia to walk out the bathroom completely naked. Yes, he had seen her body several times over the last couple of days… had even pleasured her body… but after the way she'd hidden herself early before her bath, he hadn't expected her to do this.

Taredd had just told Dain that they would meet him downstairs shortly, when he turned around to see her saunter out of the bathroom completely naked, stopping inches away from him.

Taredd could see all the cuts and bruise on her skin, but none of that seemed to bother her as she stood in front of him with desire swimming in her eyes.

Without saying a word, she raised her arms and placed her hands on the back of his head, hooking her fingers together so she could pull his face down to hers. Letting her take the lead, he let her guide him to where she wanted. She tentatively brushed her lips against his at first, then deepened the kiss.

Taredd wrapped his arms around her back and pulled her body flush against his as he met her kiss for kiss. Running his hands over her soft skin, Taredd nudged her with his hips.

Breaking the kiss, Natalia looked up into his eyes and pushed him back against the door. Taredd watched as she loosened his trousers, releasing his erect cock in the process.

As she slid his trousers down his legs, she followed them down until she was on her knees in front of him. Stepping out of the trousers, he kicked them to the side so they didn't get in the way.

As soon as he was finished and stood in front of her again, Natalia took hold of his cock with both hands. Taredd couldn't drag his eyes away from her as her petite hands gently caressed up and down his length. He watched as her tongue snaked out to lick her lips before biting her bottom lip between her teeth.

"You are so fucking beautiful," he said huskily, cupping her face in his hand.

She smiled at him before turning her attention back to his cock. Without stopping her hands, she leaned in and flicked her tongue out, tasting him with the tip of her tongue before opening her mouth wider and slowly licking around the head of his cock.

Taredd groaned as she grew more confident, her wet mouth circling the tip of his cock. Natalia gently sucked and licked the tip of his cock a few times before taking it further into her mouth.

Once she had taken as much in her mouth as she possibly could, she pulled back again until only the tip remained in her mouth. She slowly repeated the motion, torturing him with every stroke until he thought he was going to go insane.

Taredd eyes were glued to Natalia as he watched her take more and more of his cock further down her throat as she grew more relaxed. She managed to get a good rhythm going, and he was happy to let her go as far as she wanted to.

Taredd wasn't going to push her for more than she could take, so he tried to keep his hips as still as possible. Sliding in and out of her mouth with more ease as his pre-come and her saliva coated his cock.

He was finding it increasingly harder not to move his hips in time with her mouth, it was only the thought of accidentally hurting her that held him in place, but there was only so much more he could take.

Releasing his cock with one of her hands, she moved it lower down so she could cup his balls, massaging them in time with her mouth, and that did it for him. He couldn't take any more without taking over and fucking her mouth, so he pulled out of her mouth, gently pushing her away.

When she went to complain, he said: "If I don't pull out now, then I'm going to come in your mouth."

Nodding her understanding, she moved away from him. But before she had a chance to move too far away from him, Taredd picked her up and carried her over to the bed. Laying down next to her, he kissed her passionately.

Leaning all his weight on one arm, he slid his free hand to her breasts. Gently massaging her breast and playing with her nipples one and then the other until she was begging for more, pushing her breasts up invitingly.

Accepting the invitation, Taredd broke the kiss and moved to one of her breasts. Flicking his tongue over the peaked nipple before sucking it into his mouth. Gently scrapping his teeth against the sensitive peak as he pulled his head back and making a popping sound at the end.

Sliding his hand down her stomach, Taredd gently spread her legs so he had better access to the bundle of nerves hiding there. He lightly brushed his fingers over the nerves before sliding them back and dipping them inside her wet pussy.

When he pulled his finger back out, it was covered in her juices.

"Mmm... you're so wet for me," he said huskily, looking up at her from her breasts.

Natalia lifted her hips in answer, chasing his hand as he lifted it up to his face so he could suck his finger into his mouth as she watched him. Returning his hand a moment later, but instead of going where she wanted him to, he lightly traced his fingers up one thigh and down the other, getting closer and closer to her pussy with each pass.

"You taste so good," he told her.

"Please," she begged him.

"Please what?" he asked even though he knew what she wanted.

"More," she begged.

"More what?" he asked, still tormenting her with his gently touch.

Taredd wasn't going to give in so quickly. Natalia

didn't know what she was getting herself into when she started this, but she was going to find out. Taredd wanted her to tell him what she wanted him to do, and he was quite happy tormenting her until she did.

"Please, I need..."

"What do you need?" he asked before adding: "You have to tell me what you want Natalia, otherwise I'm going to carry on with what I'm doing."

Moaning, she finally gave in and said "I need your fingers."

"Where do you need them?"

"Inside me," she told him.

Giving her what she wanted at last, Taredd slid his finger back inside of her again, pumping it in and out a couple of times and making Natalia rock her hips with the motion. When he pulled it out this time, lubed with her juices, his finger slid over the bundle of nerves effortlessly.

He circled a couple of times and then slid it back inside her. Taredd repeated the action until Natalia was panting and begging for more. Only then did he crawl down the bed.

"You're so fucking wet for me," he told her.

Natalia moaned as he spread open her lips with his thumbs so he could see her pussy better.

"Fuck me," he said. "I can't wait until my cock is buried deep in here."

Pushing both his thumbs inside her, showing her what he wanted.

"Do you want that too?" he asked her.

"Yes," she said, breathlessly.

"Yes what?" he asked.

"Yes please."

"That's not the answer I was looking for Natalia," he told her. "You know what I'm wanting to hear."

"Yes, I want you inside me," she moaned.

"What do you want inside of you?" he asked. "Do you want my fingers?"

"Yes."

"How about my cock?"

"Yes, yes."

"Sounds like you really want my cock," he told her.

"Please," she begged.

"Soon," he told her. "Soon. First, I want to play... I want to taste... " he trailed off as he leaned in to lick the bundle of nerves.

Natalia moaned as she tried to get closer to his face, but Taredd moved away before she could. Using a thumb and forefinger, he held her lips open so he could watch his finger slide in and out of her pussy a couple of times before he finally leaned in and devoured her.

Just like the first time, he needed to make sure she was prepared for his size before he could slide his cock into her. Only this time, he was going to take his time.

At the back of his mind, Taredd remembered that Dain was still waiting for them downstairs. Not that Taredd cared much, it wasn't as if Dain wouldn't leave him waiting if their roles were reversed. In fact, he has done many times, so it was only right that Taredd made him wait now.

Mentally shaking any thoughts of Dain out of his mind, because he really didn't want to think of his friend while he was fucking Natalia with his fingers. So, putting Dain out of his mind, he added a third and then a forth finger. Going slowly at first so that she could adjust to the thickness of each one being added, then he sped up.

It didn't take long for Natalia to tip over the edge, her walls squeezing his fingers as she climaxed. Taredd continued fucking her with his fingers until she came back down to earth. Then, pulling them out of her, he licked her juices from them before climbing back up the bed to hover above her.

Nudging her entrance with his cock, he waited for her to look in his eyes before impaling her in one swift move of his hips. Sucking in a breath, Taredd stayed still while Natalia lifted her legs up and wrapped them around his waist, opening herself up more for him.

Leaning down, Taredd took her mouth in a fiery kiss as he started to move. Slowly at first, in a gentle rocking motion.

But when Natalia begged: "Harder... Faster," he was unable to resist, she was telling him what she wanted without any coaxing from him.

Taredd sped up until he was giving her all he had, fucking her as fast and hard as she could take. For a second, he was worried he was going to hurt her, but only for a second.

All doubt fled his mind as she shouted: "Yes! More! Yes!" as he pounded harder into her.

Pulling out suddenly, he didn't give her a chance to

complain as he quickly spun her around on to all fours and slid straight back in. In this position, he could give her the 'more' she was begging for.

Taredd could see her breasts bouncing underneath her, tormenting him as he fucked her. So, reaching his hands around her, he massaged her breasts and played with her nipples. When she started to fall to the bed, he released her breasts and grabbed hold of her hips. He held her in place as he took her harder, faster, and deeper than he had before.

The sounds coming from Natalia as he fucked her, was music to his ears and encouraged him on. Just as he could feel her walls tightening around his cock, telling him she was about to climax again, he reached around her with one hand and rubbed her clit.

A moment later, Natalia plummeted over the edge, taking him along with her.

CHAPTER THIRTY-SEVEN

Natalia

Natalia didn't regret seducing Taredd. Not for one second. How could she when he brought such pleasure to her body? She couldn't, and she didn't want to either.

If it was up to her, she would quite happily stay in this bed with him for the rest of her life, but that wasn't possible. She needed to get back to Amberly, Donovan, and the rest of the group.

So instead, she settled for whatever small amount of time with him she could get. Not knowing when they would have time alone together again, if she ever got the chance again, then she couldn't let this opportunity go without at least giving it a try.

Natalia had never felt as safe and secure in her life as what she felt laying nestled in Taredd's arms. She had never cuddled with any of her past lovers after she'd had sex with them. She didn't know if it was because it was Taredd or if she would have felt this way with anyone else, but she had a feeling it was because of Taredd though.

"We need to get going," Taredd told her, breaking

the comfortable silence. "Dain's waiting for us downstairs."

"I know, I heard you talking to Dain when I was in the bathroom," she admitted.

Taredd laughed. "So, you thought it'd be a good idea to make him wait longer?"

"No... it's just..."

"Just what?" he asked, brushing her hair from her face so he could see her better.

"I just wanted to spend a little bit more time with you before we left," Natalia didn't want to lie to him, or keep anything secret, so she told him the truth. "This might be the last time we're alone together."

"This isn't the last time we'll be alone together, I promise you," he said, lifting her face so she had to look up at him. Lightly kissing her on the tip of the nose, he added "I plan on spending a lot of time alone with you, just the two of us. But first, we have to find Arun and your friends and get back to my home... our home."

Natalia got a warm tingly feeling inside when he said it was their home. As much as the bunkers had served their purpose, none of them had even been a home.

"I hope it doesn't take too long to find them," she said.

"Me too," he said. "But it's going to take us even longer if we don't get going soon."

"Yeah, I know," she said. "Just five more minutes?"

"Okay," he told her, kissing her nose again. "But only five."

Snuggling into Taredd, Natalia enjoyed their last couple of minutes peace together, but all too soon it was time to get up and ready to leave. Natalia quickly jumped in the bath to quickly wash herself before pulling on the new clothing Dain brought for her. Natalia was glad she hadn't emptied it after her bath earlier, because she didn't have the time to run a fresh one.

It was the first time in her life that she'd ever had new clothing to wear. Normally, she had to make do with whatever she could find that would fit her while they were out scavenging.

"Ready," she said, walking back out of the bathroom fully dressed this time.

Looking her up and down, Taredd asked: "Is the size okay?"

"Yes, thank you," she said, looking down at herself. "Dain did a good job at guessing my size."

"That would be because I told him what size to get you," he told her.

"Oh," she said, blushing. "Well... thank you for getting it right."

"You are more than welcome. Shall we get going then?" he asked.

"Yes," Natalia replied as she followed him over to the door.

"Have you got everything you want?"

Looking back at the remains of her tattered clothing, she nodded.

"Yeah, I have everything I need in my satchel," she said, patting it at the same time.

"Okay, let's go."

Taredd lead her back downstairs to the large open room where they had dinner a couple of nights ago. Natalia couldn't get over how much had changed for her since she first walked into this room. Most of it was good, but she would rather forget about the part where the other Demons had grabbed her.

Dain was sat waiting at the bar for them when they joined him. Natalia couldn't help the blush from forming when he asked: "What took you two so long?"

But luckily, Taredd took the blame. "I wanted to have a bath before we left."

"And it took you that long?" Dain asked, his brows raised.

"Yes, do you have a problem with that?"

"Nope, not a damn thing," Dain said, shaking his head.

Natalia could see the smile that creep across Dain's face. She had a feeling he knew exactly why they had taken so long, but thankfully he didn't comment on it.

"So, you two finally ready to hit the road?" Dain asked, clapping his hands together.

"Yep, so hurry up and finish your drink," Taredd told him.

Dain didn't need to be told twice. Picking up his nearly full glass, he drained the lot in seconds.

Slamming his glass on the counter when it was empty, he said: "Come on then, let's go."

Taredd took Natalia's hand as they followed Dain outside and over to where he had the horses tied up. The cart was hooked up and ready to go as well.

Natalia could see that Dain had loaded the back of the cart. She wondered what he might have packed for their trip, because it was a hell of a lot more than she was used to traveling with.

When they reached the cart, Taredd grabbed her around the waist and lifted her up effortlessly. He sat her gently on one side of the bench before walking round the other side to take his own seat.

"Did you get a cover for the cart?" Taredd asked as Dain climbed onto the back of the cart.

"Yeah, but I could only get one that stretches straight across, so we'll have to only use it when no one is sitting in the back," Dain told him.

"That should be okay," Taredd said, looking at the bed of the cart. "As long as you can't see what's in there when it's covered, it'll be fine."

"No, you can't," Dain told him. "I checked it out already to make sure."

Natalia didn't see why it was so important to have a cover, but she was sure they had a good reason for it.

"Good," he said, then looked at her and asked "are you ready?"

"Yes," she told him, nervous but excited all the same.

Taredd winked at her before turning his attention back on the horses.

With a flick of the reins, he said: "Walk on."

With a jolt, the cart started moving along the cobbled street. The click-clacking of the horses hooves on the cobbles soon stopped once they were on a dirt road.

Natalia wasn't sure if she like this form of travel or not. It was a lot bumpier than she thought it was going to be, but she supposed it beat the hell out of walking. Especially since she didn't know how far they needed to travel.

"You get used to it after a while," Dain said from behind her, making her jump.

"Oh... it's okay," she told him.

"You should have picked up some cushions for Natalia to sit on," Taredd told him.

"Yeah, in hindsight, I probably should have," Dain said. "We can always turn back."

Taredd looked over at Natalia.

"Do you want us to turn back for some?" he asked her.

"No, it's okay, I promise," she assured them both.

"Well, I'll tell you what, we'll pick some up in the next town we pass," he told her.

"You don't need to," Natalia told him again. "I promise, it's fine."

Taredd thought about it for a minute, then shook his head and said: "No, we'll get some at the next town. This bench will get even more uncomfortable after a long time sitting on it, especially with all the bumps when we travel off a paved road."

"Okay," she told him.

Natalia didn't see what the problem was until they left the smooth paving onto rough uneven earth and had been traveling that way for an hour. By the time they finally stopped, Natalia had lost all feeling in her ass. Natalia was more than ready to get off the cart to stretch her legs when Taredd pulled the horses to a halt.

"I think we'll stop here for the night," he said. "It's starting to get dark and we need to get a fire going for Natalia to stay warm."

"It's okay by me," Dain said as he jumped off the back of the cart.

"I don't mind if you want to keep going," Natalia told them.

"No, we should stop for something to eat and to give the horses a rest," Taredd told her. "Plus, you need to sleep at some point."

"Yeah, we definitely need to stop for food. I'm fucking starving," Dain said.

"I could always sleep in the back of the cart if you want to keep going through the night," Natalia offered.

"You'll be sleeping there anyway," Taredd told her. "Just not while we're traveling. It would be too uncomfortable otherwise, and you would wake up in pain, if you managed to get any sleep at all."

"Oh," Natalia said, unsure what else to say to that.

"Don't worry, there's a rolled-up mattress under one of the benches, so it'll be comfy enough," Dain told her.

Natalia instantly panicked about stripping during the night. If it was just like sleeping in a bed, then there was a higher chance she would strip down like she normally did.

Taredd must have read her mind, because he told her: "That's what the cover is for."

Breathing a sigh of relief, she said: "Thank you."

"You're welcome, but it's more for my sake than yours."

"I don't understand," Natalia said, and she really didn't.

"I don't want Dain to see you naked," he said, making her blush. "If he does, I'm likely to beat the shit out of him. But he's my friend, so I would rather not do that."

"Yeah, I would rather he didn't as well," Dain added.

"Oh, I see," Natalia said, blushing. "Thank you."

Natalia was grateful Taredd had remembered what she did while she was asleep. He didn't judge her for it either, like some of the people in her group had done in the past. He accepted it was just something she did and that she couldn't stop herself from doing it.

That's when it dawned on her... she was falling in love with a Demon... she was falling in love with Taredd.

CHAPTER THIRTY-EIGHT

Taredd

Taredd was very grateful that Dain had managed to scrape together everything they could have possibly needed for the long trip ahead, except for some cushions for Natalia to sit on that is. He even picked up items for Natalia that Taredd would never have even considered getting for her.

Clearing the back of the cart, Taredd made space so that he could roll out the mattress for Natalia to sleep on. While he was doing that, Dain made a start on putting the cover over the top half. Natalia asked if she could help, but both Taredd and Dain told her to rest.

Natalia didn't listen to either of them though. Instead, she helped by gathering some firewood and piling it up against a tree.

"Right," Dain said when he was finished. "I'll get a fire going so we can cook some dinner."

"Did you bring something to cook? Or do you want me to set a trap and catch something?" Taredd asked him.

"Nah, save your traps for another night," Dain said, pointing to the bags. "There's plenty of food in one of them."

"Which one?" Taredd asked.

"I don't fucking know, have a look, it's in one of them," Dain told him.

Rummaging through the bags, Taredd grumbled: "It would be a lot easier if you knew which one it was packed in."

"Next time I'll make sure to label all the bags, okay? Now stop bitching and find it already," Dain said as he picked up all of the firewood Natalia had collected, and dumped it in a pile in the middle of the small clearing they had stopped next to.

"Oh, yes please," Taredd said sarcastically. "That would be absolutely fantastic, thank you."

"Do you two always bitch at each other like this?" Natalia asked them.

"No," they said in unison.

"Normally it's Dain and Arun bitching at each other, but I think Dain's missing Arun so he's starting with me," Taredd told her.

"That's bullshit," Dain said. "Me and Arun don't bitch all the time. Taredd just thinks we do."

"That's because you do," Taredd told him.

"No, we just like to irritate the fuck out of you, that's all," Dain said, smiling.

"Don't I know it," Taredd said, shaking his head.

"Why do you like irritating Taredd?" Natalia asked Dain.

"Because it's fun, why else?" Dain said, with a big cheesy grin on his face.

Taredd could see Natalia out of the corner of his eye

smiling back at Dain, but she still told him: "That's mean."

"Nah, it's not," Dain said. "You'll see, it's fun I promise."

It wasn't news to Taredd. He already knew that they did it on purpose the majority of the time, which was why it pissed him off so much. They couldn't spend one single day together without bitching about something or other.

In fact, this had been the longest he'd gone without listening to them, and that was only because Arun wasn't here.

Finally finding the bag with the food in it, Taredd pulled out what they needed for tonight and left the rest in the bag. It didn't take long for Dain to get the fire going.

Natalia sat on the floor with her legs crossed in front of her. She was as close to the fire as she could get without being burned, or risking her clothing catching on fire. Taredd would have preferred her to be a little further away, but with how cold it was out tonight, he knew she was just trying to stay warm.

After passing Dain all the food, Taredd went back to rummaging in the bags. Pulling out a blanket from one of them, he walked over and wrapped it around Natalia.

"Thank you," she said, smiling up at him as she pulled it tighter around her.

"You're welcome," he told her.

Dain watched them out of the corner of his eye. Taredd knew he was trying to be discrete about it, but

Taredd could tell he was watching how they were interacting.

Once Natalia was asleep later that night, Taredd knew Dain was going to ask if he intended on mating with Natalia. A week ago, he would have laughed in Dain's face at the mention of mating with a Human. Now, he was more than eager to seal the deal with Natalia, tying her life to his for all eternity.

But before that could happen, he needed to speak with her. There was no way he would mate with her if it wasn't something that she wanted. He hadn't asked her if she had a mate... or husband as the Humans called it... because at first, he hadn't cared. Then after they spent the night together, he was afraid to ask for fear the answer was yes.

Now though, he had no choice. He wanted... needed... to know that she was his and his alone. Only then would he bring up the subject of mating with her.

He also needed to speak with Arun to see if there was anything, he could do with his magic to extend Natalia's life to that of his own. Otherwise he would eventually lose her. There was no way in hell he was going to let that happen.

If Arun couldn't help him, then he would search all the realms for someone who could.

Epilogue

Natalia woke up to the sound of Taredd calling her name and gently shaking her.

With a groan, Natalia said groggily: "I'm awake."

"Open your eyes and I might believe you," Taredd told her.

Without even seeing his face, Natalia could tell that he was smiling at her.

Peeking at him through one eye, she said: "There you go, my eyes are open."

"Both eyes." He laughed at her.

"But it's too early," she moaned.

"No, it's not," he told her. "Dain and I have been up for hours."

"Yeah, but knowing you two, you've probably been up all night and not slept at all."

"True," he agreed. "But still, it's time to get up. We need to find Arun and your friends."

The reminder of her friends did it. Opening both eyes, she looked at him as she stretched under the blanket.

Grateful she hadn't stripped in her sleep again, she sat up when Dain reached over the side of the cart to pass her a cup with steam billowing out of it.

"Here, this will wake you up," he told her.

"What is it?" she asked, pulling a face as she sniffed the contents.

"It's just coffee, it won't poison you."

Natalia had heard about coffee, but she had never tried it before. Normally she drank herbal teas from whatever herbs they found growing close to where they were staying at the time.

"It's good," Dain said.

"It doesn't smell very good," she told him.

"Yeah, it tastes better than it smells though," Dain said, pulling a face of his own.

"Try it," Taredd told her. "If nothing else, it'll wake you up."

"Fine, but if it's nasty, I'm gonna spit it at you," she said, pointing at Dain.

"Why me?" he asked with a shocked expression on his face.

"Because you handed it to me," she told him.

"Taredd told me to," he told her. "So, if you are going to spit it at anyone, it should be him."

"Natalia, trust me, you'll like it," Taredd told her. "You've liked everything else so far, haven't you."?

"Yeah, you're right," she told him. She added: "Okay, I trust you." Then took a sip.

"Nice?" Taredd asked her.

"It's not too bad actually," she said, honestly.

"See, I told you," he said. "Now drink up, because we have to get going soon."

"Do you want some breakfast?" Dain asked her.

"Urm... yes please," Natalia said. "That's if we have

enough time."

"Of course," Taredd said.

"There's always time for food," Dain added with a grin on his face.

Smiling back at him, she said: "Well then, yes please, I would love some breakfast."

Before she had a chance to move, Dain passed her a plate filled with bread, cheese, and cooked meat. She would have to get up soon enough, but for the time being, she was happy just to sit there being waited on hand and foot.

Having breakfast in bed was a first for her, and she had to admit, it was really nice. Never in her wildest dreams did she ever imagine a Demon and a Shapeshifter would be the ones to make her breakfast in bed for the first time.

Natalia could definitely get used to being treated like this. She may not be in a real bed, but it was still technically the same thing. It was just outside among nature instead of being cooped up inside a room.

As soon as Natalia was finished eating, she climbed down from the cart. Beelining it to a small stream not too far from where they had set up camp. She washed as best as she could before joining Taredd and Dain by the cart again.

"You ready to go?" Taredd asked her as she walked up to him.

"Yes.”

"Good,” he said, smiling down at her.

Smiling back, she accepted his help again to get back onto the cart. Natalia sat up front next to Taredd again, while Dain sprawled out in the back, snoring his head off. Natalia didn't know how anyone could sleep with the number of bumps they were going over.

They hadn't travelled that far before Natalia suddenly shouted: "Stop!"

"What's the matter?" Taredd asked as he brought the horses to a halt.

"There's a bunker over there," she said, pointing into the woods.

"Are you sure?" Dain asked. "Because I don't see anything."

"Yes, I'm positive," she told him.

Jumping down from the cart, Natalia walked off in the direction she had spotted the circular man hole cover that was used for a door, leaving Taredd and Dain no choice but to follow after her or wait at the cart. She didn't really care if they came with her or not.

Natalia shouldn't have been able to see it clearly from the road, but someone had left it open. It was probably to let some fresh air inside, but there was also the possibility that they had just forgotten to close it after themselves.

Either way, Natalia was going to have a word with whoever is in there. Simple mistakes like that could risk everyone else's lives.

As soon as the entrance came into view again, Natalia raced over to the entrance. Taredd grabbed her around the waist before she could swing her leg over the side, stopping her from climbing down the ladder.

"What are you doing?" she asked before demanding "Let go of me."

"Natalia, do your kind usually leave this open?" he asked, pointing at the open doorway.

"No, they don't," she told him. "I plan on having a word with whoever left it open though, because they all know better than that."

"Dain, check it out down there please," Taredd said, still holding tight to Natalia.

"On it," Dain said, swiftly leaping over the side, not bothering to use the ladder.

"Why?" Natalia asked.

"Because something isn't right," he told her.

"What do you mean something isn't right? What's wrong?" she asked worriedly.

"I'm not sure yet, but there's something off about this," he said, pointing at the open door.

Natalia had a feeling Taredd knew more than he was letting on, but she didn't question him further. But when Dain returned, she knew that Taredd was right by the look on his face.

"What is it? What's happened?" Natalia asked.

Shaking his head, Dain said "No one is here."

"I don't believe you," she said, watching as the men shared a look.

Looking back at her, Dain said "I promise, Natalia, there is no one here."

"Let go of me," she told Taredd.

He hesitated a moment, but did as she asked, releasing her from his hold.

"Now, get out my way," she told Dain. "I'm going down there whether you like it or not."

Dain looked at Taredd, who nodded to do what she

asked. He climbed out the rest of the way and moved to the side, leaving her enough room to get past.

As soon as he was clear, Natalia climbed down the ladder. At first glance, everything looked as it should. A little messy, but mostly fine. It wasn't until she walked in the bedroom that she saw what Dain was trying to prevent her from seeing.

A large puddle of blood covered half the bedroom floor. Her heart instantly sank and tears welled up in her eyes, making everything blurry.

"No..." She said, dropping to her knees. "It can't be them."

She vaguely heard Taredd climb down the ladder, but she was too consumed with grief and guilt to pay him any attention.

Please don't let it be Amberly and Donovan. She prayed silently, over and over again as the tears fell unchecked down her cheeks.

***

Natalia was on her knees when he reached the back room where the beds were. He could hear her crying and it pained him. Taredd would do anything to take away her pain, but looking around the bunker Taredd knew without a doubt that something bad had happened here, and recently as well. The puddle of blood was still fresh on the floor.

"We've got to find Amberly and Donovan!" Natalia suddenly said as she jumped up and raced towards the ladder.

"Wait," Taredd said as he grabbed her around the waist as she went to pass him.

"No! Let go of me!" She shouted as tears streamed down her face, fighting to get free of his hold.

"Natalia, listen to me," Taredd said, spinning her so she faced him. Only once she was looking at him did he continue. "Whoever did this could still be in the area."

"I don't care!" She said as her voice broke. "I need to find them."

"We will, I promise," he told her pulling her tight against his chest as she sobbed. "Dain..."

"I'm on it," he said, knowing what Taredd wanted him to do.

"I can't lose them, they're like a brother and sister to me."

"We will find them, Natalia," Taredd said.

Whether they were alive or not was another matter. He hoped for her sake they were alive, but with the amount of blood in the other room, it was highly unlikely. More than one person died in that room for sure. Who it was, was anyone's guess.

Maybe if Taredd or Dain had met them before this happened, they would be able to know from the scents in the room. Having never met them, that made it impossible for them to know.

Dain took his time searching the area. Natalia didn't leave Taredd's arms the entire time Dain was gone, not even to pack up anything that might belong to her friends.

When he finally returned, he said "It's all clear

outside. Whoever was here, they're long gone."

The small glimmer of hope he saw in Natalia's eyes at seeing Dain return, was dashed the moment those words left his mouth.

"It's going to be okay, Natalia, Dain is the best at tracking. Aren't you Dain?" Taredd said, trying to give her some reassurance.

"That's right. Don't worry, Natalia, we will find them, I promise."

"You don't think it's your other friend, do you?" she asked them.

"What? Arun?" Taredd asked.

"Yes."

"No, it's definitely not him."

"How do you know that for sure?"

"Because, first off, he's not a very good hunter, so he's probably still out there trying to find one of your kind," Dain told her. "And second, the only way to win the bet, is to capture a human alive. It would negate the bet if the human was dead. For all we know, it could just be one someone else killed."

"And there's no way Arun would let me win the bet on a technicality," Taredd told her.

Which was true, Arun would rather lose than cheat, or be seen as cheating. Not only that, but Arun preferred a clean kill, and what happened here was far from clean. So, Taredd was positive it wasn't Arun.

"I promise you, we will not stop looking until we find them." It may be the biggest mistake of his life, but dead or alive, he was going to reunite Natalia with her friends, even if it was the last thing he did.

To Be Continued

Dear reader

I hope you enjoyed reading this book as much as I
enjoyed writing it.
Please could you take a moment to leave a review,
even if it's only a line or two, about what you thought
of the book.
Also, if you'd like to know about upcoming new
releases, sneak-peeks, and special offers you can sign
up to my newsletter. You can also find me on
Facebook and Goodreads.

Thank you and much love.

Georgina.

You can find my newsletter sign-up here:
https://mailchi.mp/70d528570834/georginastancer

Printed in Great Britain
by Amazon

55721233R00163